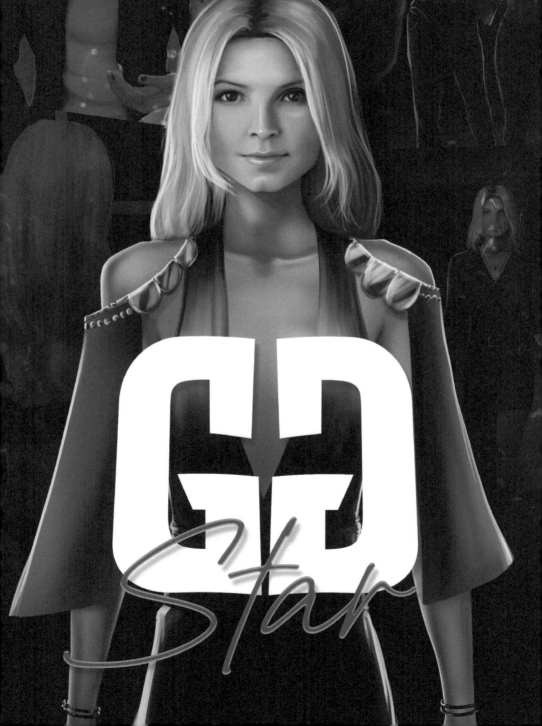

VALENTINA DZHERSON

GG
Star

Prende Publishing
Las Vegas ◊ Chicago ◊ Palm Beach

Published in the United States of America by
Histria Books
7181 N. Hualapai Way, Ste. 130-86
Las Vegas, NV 89166 USA
HistriaBooks.com

Prende Publishing is an imprint of Histria Books. Titles published under the imprints of Histria Books are distributed worldwide.

Library of Congress Control Number: 2024931029

ISBN 978-1-59211-422-1 (softbound)
ISBN 978-1-59211-439-9 (eBook)

C O N T E N T S

※

PART 1

The History of the Universe

※

Chapter 1

THE GREAT BALANCE

Millions of years ago, before humankind existed, there was a wide universe in which Light and Dark Energy collided. No one knows where these two opposing energies originated from, but they were strong enough to create every galaxy and celestial object, as well as our planet.

Light and Dark Energy coexist in what is called the Great Balance, and one cannot be without the other. Together, these energy forces maintain balance and bring harmony to every being in the universe. The Great Balance is not a combination of good and evil. While it is difficult to understand, the Great Balance describes two equally powerful energies that can symbolize good and evil in our world. One cannot understand good without evil, and vice versa.

In the universe, every element has a purpose, each with its own strength and weakness. Together, all the elements generate massive power despite their differences. They compensate each other and make the universe function as it's supposed to.

The last thing the Great Balance created was planet Earth. This universal conscience knew this planet would be inhabited by a diverse life: people, animals, plants, and other various microorganisms. However, life is fragile and needs a patron who will look after and protect it, keeping order and justice. A patron would see that the power of the Great Balance on Earth functions correctly and proportionally. Thus, the Balance created God as the main manager of the equal forces of Light and Dark Energy.

God was one for everyone and everything. Even if humans asked or begged him, He did not punish or reward. He neither killed, nor resurrected. He gave nothing and took nothing away. God did not work miracles and did not do evil, regardless of what people begged Him for. God only made sure that the power of the Great Balance on Earth worked, and that every being on the planet did what it was supposed to do. Earth prospered, grew, and developed.

In the time of the Great Balance, people were not afraid of death. They lived and were grateful for their life. When they were near death, they knew that they had already completed their mission on the planet and their passing would make room for a new life. Their bodies were destroyed, but their souls would get to live in a new body with a new mission. No one died completely; instead, there was a rebirth, which is why no one cried at funerals. Death is how the Great Balance recycled human life.

People were not afraid of poverty. They learned to make do with what they had, and if they did not have enough, they learned to acquire new skills to get what they lacked, by trial and error. People did not blame anyone for their failures. When faced with failure, they knew that they were not putting in enough effort, or perhaps they were dealing with evil.

Evil didn't look the same to everyone, and what is good for a person now could become evil for them tomorrow. It depended on how a person acted and what they believed in. The same good or the same evil could change places depending on circumstances. There was no constancy in them, but together they created balance, which kept peace and love in the people's lives. Good and Evil complemented each other like day and night, and together they moved towards progress and evolution. Both were important, and both were irreplaceable. A person could not have a clear mind and strong body to work hard during the daytime if they did not have the rest gained at night. Like day and night, good and evil each fulfilled its function.

In the time of the Great Balance, no one was ever jealous of physical beauty. People knew that everyone had a type. Physical beauty standards did not exist. Society did not dictate which appearance was beautiful and which was not. Beauty was in the eye of the beholder. People knew that inner beauty was most important. The most beautiful people were blessed with qualities like kindness, love, care, support, understanding, generosity, and empathy. Without internal beauty, external beauty is just an attractive shell, even if it still needs to be respected for the effort put into it.

People never sought to steal, kill, or offend one another on purpose. They knew that the karma works strictly according to the Great Balance system, and they received exactly what they gave. Simply put, all energy sent would be returned. People understood that if they wanted good for themselves, they should be kind to other people, animals, and nature. They wished well for themselves, so they treated other people kindly, living in peace and harmony. Back then, there was never any war. The Great Balance taught them that the pleasure of victory was not enough to compensate for what was lost during the battle. Thus, people learned the art of negotiation and diplomacy. They knew how expensive wars were when it came to economy and energy.

Everyone enjoyed not only receiving love, but how it made them feel when they loved in return. If they needed love, they would offer it to others. The Great Balance showed them that loving others started with loving themselves first, and the strongest form of love is the one given without expecting anything in return. There were never any broken hearts, as people loved sincerely without any expectation or hope. They gave love freely and openly, enjoying its warmth. Love was pure and healing. Forced love was sure to turn into hate, and hate killed from the inside and would break their own hearts. They never blamed anyone who loved back, as the Great Balance showed how people were able to hurt themselves by expectations that were never promised.

Importantly, the Great Balance showed people that happiness depended on themselves. No one gifted a person with happiness. One had to first learn to be happy in their own company. Happiness came with the effort of training one's mind to think positively, enjoy the present moment, be here and now, and not think about the past or the future. When not living in the present, people had much to lose. Of course, once a person knew happiness, they would share it with others.

People were very relaxed about success. They were able to accept the idea that success had a very different meaning to each person. For some, success meant money, while for others, it meant a career. For some, it was their loving family, and for others, it was just the simple act of breaking bad habits or learning how to play the piano. The Great Balance made sure not a single person could dictate the best or right model of success. Goals and success were different for everyone.

In the time of the Great Balance, people valued health over physical beauty, money, or success because the Great Balance showed them that without health, they could not enjoy life properly. Neither money, sex, or food could replace a strong immune system. Learning from experience, people concluded that they could not be truly happy and full of vital energy if they were sick. Good health was important, and it was one of people's main values: to preserve and strengthen both physical and mental health. Just as good and evil complimented each other, a healthy body complimented a healthy mind.

In terms of nature, people loved and respected their environment. They understood that they had to take care of nature because they used its resources and without it, they would not survive. Sometimes people behaved selfishly concerning nature, but when this happened, nature reprimanded them with hurricanes, fires, floods, crop failures, and other natural disasters. These forces of nature taught people to properly cherish and respect nature's gifts. Once people learned this lesson, the relationship between people and nature became harmonious.

All knew how important it was to have friends. Friendships were valued as much as family and were very strong, usually from childhood and throughout life. Friendships were sincere, based mainly on the attraction of one soul to another and regardless of the difference in age, social status, or nationality. People were friends for the sake of being friends. They had fun in the company of others and shared secrets and experiences, cared for each other, and helped one another.

In the time of the Great Balance, people had respect for their sexuality. They understood that this was a very important area of their life and health. People studied their own sexuality and that of their partner with care. A healthy, full-fledged sex life added happiness and joy, while increasing self-esteem and self-confidence. Plus, it gave additional energy to the development of business and new ideas. People understood that sexual energy was very strong and productive, and like a magnet, it attracted good luck and opportunities.

Sexually satisfied people appeared happy, attractive, charming, and friendly, and therefore easily adapted to society or in a new environment. Everyone understood how important it was to cherish their sexuality, which propelled them forward in life and gave them strength. People were very respectful and tolerant of other people's sexual energy and orientation. It was obvious that the libido of different people was not the same. This difference was normal as it was intended by nature. Going against one's sexuality meant fighting one's own nature, and it was harmful to people's mental and physical health.

People understood the value of the inner energy resources they possessed. They were not afraid and did not hesitate to ask for help and support from each other when they needed it. The energy charge of a strong personality was so powerful that it was able to heal the mental wounds of others, inspire discouraged people, warm cold hearts, and fill weakened people with energy through hugs and physical touch. The most powerful medicine was kindness and acceptance. People had tremendous empathy for each other and respected emotional health. They understood the value of an internal energy charge. When a person was full of strength and vital energy, they could share it with others. They

would not be depleted by sharing it, but on the contrary: the one who gives gets even more.

When people made mistakes, such as knowingly or deliberately injuring each other with words or actions, the energetic charge of both was exhausted and they both felt powerless, dejected, and ashamed. Even if a person won but hurt the feelings of the other in the process, they still felt bad and lost energy that needed to be filled. The power of the Great Balance helped people understand that they should treat other people as well as they treat themselves. Otherwise, they would lose their vitality and consume the energy of the people whom they hurt by words or actions. Therefore, people did not want to offend others, and people sought to help others because, through the help and support of others, they also automatically helped themselves.

Lastly, people knew how to rejoice at the success of others. In this way, confidence in their strength and their success multiplied. Sometimes when people were jealous or contributing to other people's failures, they themselves failed or lost. People understood that wherever they directed their energy for good or evil, that's where it would increase and grow. Through experience, people learned more and more lessons, and thus the power of the Great Balance kept the equal forces of good and evil under control. There was much good, but sometimes there was also evil. People needed both good and evil to lead fulfilled lives.

Life on Earth developed at a rapid pace. Paradise existed on Earth, and God looked after the Light and Dark energies, making sure they were equally distributed as instructed by the Great Balance. However, one day, something went wrong.

※

Chapter 2

DARK ENERGY

No one knows what exactly happened, but for some reason, The Great Balance was disturbed and the power of Dark Energy began to grow faster than Light Energy. Dark Energy began to fill the entire outer space and gradually reached the planet Earth. The stars of the galaxy, like all other planets, remained in their places and functioned unchanged. But planet Earth was the most fragile and sensitive, and therefore subject to changes by dark forces. The living creatures that populated it had souls and hearts, which is what made the planet Earth so vulnerable and dependent on the equal forces of The Great Balance. The harmony on Earth was broken, and this began the time of The Great Imbalance.

Dark Energy spread throughout planet Earth. First, it penetrated the hearts and heads of people, violating the harmony and peace within them. Subsequently, the harmonious relationships between people in society was destroyed. Dark Energy subconsciously nurtured people's egos, and their hearts grew cold and their souls suffered. People forgot moral principles like honesty, respect, and helping their neighbors. They focused only on their personal goals and resorted to any methods for their achievement. Even if these methods brought pain and suffering to other people, they were willing to make such a selfish bargain.

Success became a trend and society began to dictate the standards of success, with money and business being the center of everything. No one cared about human feelings and emotions because everyone focused only on financial gain. The value of an individual in society was measured by their financial well-being and social status. Moral qualities no longer mattered. Personal relationships between people grew colder and turned into consumer relationships, according to the model of mutual use. The concept of kindness was deprecated and replaced with service and use. Selflessness and sincerity were equated with naivety and foolishness. The hearts of people in society became callous, their minds cold and cynical.

Human nature's kindness and gentleness lost popularity, while indifference towards one another gained momentum. The society of caring communities was no more. Now, society was only individual entrepreneurs and businessmen who kept apart. They strived for personal progress and couldn't be bothered by others, so they separated from society.

Financial success became a universal goal, and it was the single meaning of life. People began to spend all their vitality and resources on developing businesses, achieving financial success, and climbing the rungs of the social status ladder. Those who were unable to move towards their own goals were hired to work for other people to develop their businesses. As a result, society was divided into masters and slaves.

Dark Energy continued to spread faster than Light Energy, and the Light Energy that did exist was weakened. People adapted to The Great Imbalance with new mindsets, behaviors, and relationships. A new world was born, one where the power of Dark Energy ruled.

With the new trend of success and wealth, the fear of poverty and failure spread like a sickness. People were so zombified with the idea of the necessity of success at any cost that they lived with a constant fear of poverty and misery. People worked without days off or rest breaks. With fear hanging over their heads, they worked themselves to the bone in the name of achieving their goals and being successful.

Obsessed with fear, people in the time of The Great Imbalance were more and more distant from their relatives and friends. They devoted less time to hobbies and entertainment. They completely stopped hearing the inner voice of their souls, which had always told them the truth about life's purpose being about vitality and happiness. People were slaves to money, and no matter how much they worked, there was never enough money to satisfy their thirst.

The fear of poverty that swept the Earth was followed by another fear: that of death. People grew terrified of death. They could not live happily in the moment. They rushed events forward or looked back at the mistakes of the past. With their heads occupied with the past or the future, people simply could not feel the pleasure experienced in the present. They devalued the simple joys of the present moment.

While the fear of death gained momentum and the frightened minds of people began to believe in the mystical power of magical creatures that dominated humanity. People grew so cowardly that they simply did not want to take responsibility for their own destinies. The unknowns--what direction their life would take, who they would become, and how they would die--were too overwhelming to them. Therefore, people invented Gods who, they claimed, governed their lives. Since people were so frightened, their own souls were devoid of that guiding voice. People could not take responsibility for themselves and their lives, so they decided to enslave themselves to the Gods and fixed the shackles on their wrists themselves.

When the idea that the Gods control the lives of people evolved, people worked to figure out how to bribe the Gods. Since they had no control over their lives anymore, they had to obtain happiness, success, and wealth by bribing the Gods. They came up with various rituals, ceremonies, and sacrifices to honor the Gods. Thus, religion was born. Religion took root in society at the level of the law, and if someone denied or doubted the existence and power of God, they were severely punished. In this way, people relied less and less on their own strengths and more and more on the magic of deities.

Even though many believed that their lives, happiness, and success depended on God, no one had ever seen Him and people disagreed on the specifics of God. Different parts of society began to offer various ideas of how God looked, what He wore, and what God Himself believed in. So many theories arose that people began to be divided into separate social groups according to their different religious ideologies.

Dark Energy continued to fester in the air, and the people of Earth were finally no longer united. Wars, conspiracies, and the division of territories began. People turned to violence, learning the skills of fighting robbing, and killing each other. Aggression manifested itself as the best defense against attack. Therefore, pain, fear, and violence only increased. People did not understand that they were producing all this chaos.

Due to wars, competition, and aggression on Earth, the concept of love virtually disappeared. Love was recalled less and less often, since the minds of people were busy with survival and their hearts were occupied with faith and service to the Gods who should have helped them. The concept of unconditional love gradually disappeared altogether, and love became exclusively conditional.

In the time of The Great Imbalance, love was more like a mutually beneficial exchange. Love was exchanged for money, for shelter, for a position in society, or for the company of a warm body. In the rare instances of acts of unconditional love, people viewed them with suspicion. Relationships were unhealthy and co-dependent. People did not marry out of love, but out of fear of loneliness and the emotional pressure from family and society. Couples were not happy together, but continued to live together and give birth to children.

Regarding the environment, which people used to cherish and respect, there was no regard for preservation or protection. People became less sensitive to nature, and they consumed more resources. Nature began taking revenge against humankind through fires, tsunamis, hurricanes, and floods. These natural disasters were also triggered by the Earth's excessive exposure to Dark Energy.

The physical beauty of people was more and more an instrument of domination in society. This concerned women most, but men as well. It was easiest for beautiful people to obtain a higher position in society and move forward in life, so everyone tried to meet the standards of beauty that were dictated by society's elite. Cold and thoughtless obsession with physical beauty and its invented standards forced people to go against their physical natural beauty. People began to do plastic surgeries on their faces and bodies. Women enlarged their lips and breasts, completely losing their authenticity and uniqueness.

At the same time, people lost confidence in themselves. The more people artificially improved their appearance, the less they were satisfied with the result. Trying to meet the invented standard of beauty and contorting their appearance into unnatural ways, they emotionally lost themselves. By distorting their appearance, people distorted their psyche. The psyche of people became unstable, leading more and more people to have mental health issues. The pursuit of beauty standards put people's emotional and physical health at risk. People did not value their own health and risked it for the sake of being liked by society. However, no matter how many plastic surgeries they underwent, it was never close enough to perfection. People stopped loving themselves, so they were no longer able to love other people in a healthy way.

People began to feel less sexy and less powerful. At the same time, a disharmonious society filled with Dark Energy set a new standard: sex and money ruled the world. Only rich and sexy people could receive the highest social privileges. Everyone--despite being emotionally depleted, unsure of themselves, and suffering from an unstable psyche and poor health--had to meet high sexual standards, plus strong sexual energy and attractiveness.

This was not possible for everyone, but for the sake of fame, universal approval, and public admiration, people began to try to meet the new standards anyway. All they could do, with their very low internal energy resources, was be fake. This was the beginning of the total self-destruction of each individual separately and society as a whole.

While people still tried to appear happy and successful, this charade further increased their anxiety. In the midst of internal disharmony, people felt and understood their own sexuality less and less, so they did not even try to delve into or study the sexuality of their partners.

No one studied the issues of sexual communication, the nature of human sexuality, sexual development, sexual differences between people, or sexual needs. Therefore, no one really understood the art of sex and sexual techniques, so people did not have sex very often, and if they did, it was not very effective and not very pleasurable. Still, people pretended, and they falsified pleasure and sexual emotions for each other. People preferred the appearance of being a good lover than actually being one. People falsified their emotions and pretended to be who they weren't so much that they lost themselves. They no longer understood who they really were or what they wanted. People no longer listened to the voice of their souls or to the call of their hearts. People were led only by their brain, which was filled with the attitudes of social norms.

In the time of The Great Imbalance, society gradually turned into masses of insecure, lonely people with unstable psyches.They were filled with emptiness in their souls and were miserable all the time. All they could do was work, for themselves or for other people. People loved to work because only in this way could they see their success. Therefore, they worked hard.

Even after society became entrenched in its evil, Dark Energy did not cease spreading the power of its negative influence.

※

Chapter 3

THE MEETING OF THE GODS

Through a mysterious and cosmic twist of fate, when people invented Gods and religions, the Gods became real. So intense and primal was people's desperation for a higher power that the universe responded by creating the very Gods the people craved.

People were afraid of themselves, and they became hostages to their fears. They wanted to give up their own inner power and strength and have a higher power take over. People did not believe in themselves and were afraid of their own desires. They wanted benevolent Gods to control their lives and destinies, so they did.

The Gods began to rule people and decide their destinies for them in reality. However, good must be balanced by evil, so the benevolent Gods had to be balanced by anti-Gods, or Devils. Therefore, Devils came into being as well. This is how Hell appeared with all the terrible evil spirits. People created Hell with their thoughts and invented the concept of an afterlife. People endlessly worshiped Gods out of fear and asked for protection from the Devils.

In short, the people of Earth were afraid of the Gods living in Paradise and the Devils living in Hell. A beautiful, harmonious life on planet Earth had turned into a hellscape of brutal survival.

As a result of The Great Imbalance, people no longer had a source of creative energy and inspiration. They no longer lived a full life. They simply existed in distrust and loneliness, their heads full of various fears. People of all nations and religions began to intensely pray to the Gods for them to send help to Earth, so humans could return to inner peace and harmony and feel love in their hearts again.

Unbeknownst to humans, just as various nations were waging war on Earth, their Gods were also waging war. The Gods were at enmity with each other, but they also fought with the Devils and with all the evil entities that were in Hell. This was the endless battle of good versus evil. However, the situation on planet Earth was so critical that it seemed on the verge of extinction.

The Gods decided to agree to a temporary truce and meet for negotiations. They held a gathering to discuss how to help people, how to stop the spread of Dark Energy, and how to restore The Great Balance, which would lead to harmony on earth. The Devils also came to the meeting of the Gods to join their deliberations because even the Devils knew that such a great imbalance of Dark Energy was unnatural and unsustainable. If Dark Energy continued to dominate the world, Earth itself would collapse and humanity would meet its demise. If humanity was wiped out, the Gods and Devils would cease to exist, as people were the ones who brought them into being, and without their belief in them, they would disappear. So not only did the Gods and Devils plot to save humanity, they plotted to save themselves too.

At the general meeting, the Gods and Devils discussed, debated, and offered various options for who or what could save planet Earth. The main problem was that the power of The Great Imbalance was much greater than all the power of the Gods combined.

The source of the earthly problem was the unnatural proliferation of Dark Energy, which caused The Great Imbalance. This dilemma meant that the Gods and Devils had to find or create something that could restore equilibrium in the universe and bring back The Great Balance to save planet Earth.

The Gods and Devils, united in their efforts, decided to create a superhero, who would be endowed with the strength of each of them. This superhero would be tasked with saving Earth. They would create a forceful star imbued with the cosmic power of the universe that would serve as the superhero's soul. The Gods named her GG Star.

※

PART 2

*The Creation of
GG Star*

✳

Chapter 4

THE GODS BESTOW POWERS

After numerous disputes, the Gods and all the cosmic entities agreed that by uniting forces they would create a superhero named GG Star. This superhero would be endowed with divine and cosmic superpowers that would make her immune to the power of Dark Energy. In this way, GG Star would be strong enough to resist Dark Energy, champion Light Energy, and restore The Great Balance.

First, the Gods and Devils together created a special and super-strong star and endowed it with unique abilities. With both the powers of Dark Energy and Light Energy combined, the star was a perfect embodiment of The Great Balance, which the world so desperately needed.

None of the Gods, Devils, or other entities in the cosmic system knew exactly how to restore the balance on Earth and what kind of power was capable of harmonizing the world. Since disharmony led to a decline in vitality and creative energy, the Gods decided that the incredibly powerful force of sexual energy was

their best shot at saving the world and combatting The Great Imbalance. If a superhero could harness and wield the awesome power of sexual energy, they could restore the vitality of life to people and revive that inspirational creative energy the dark, dull world lacked. The superhero with the soul of a star would be granted the superpowers needed to save humanity.

The Gods and Devils decided the superhero must live among humans, so they decided to put GG Star in a human body. The divine GG Star would be facing evil in human form, and she would fight The Great Imbalance on Earth. Her goal was the inner peace and harmony of humanity through sexuality. Her main superpower was to awaken sexual desire in everyone, thanks to her potent sexual energy. If successful in her mission, GG Star would revive the people's power of life, their inner creative energy, and their natural inspiration!

When they created her, each of the Gods put his or her particular strength into GG Star, so she possessed such superpowers as:

Divine beauty so enchanting that everyone, without exception, would fall in love with her

Eternal youth, so that after reaching the age of 18, her body would stop aging

Immortality, so she could live forever until her mission was complete

The healing power of inner harmony, so powerful that she could heal people through her positive influence

Strength, so that she had the moral fortitude to resist the temptation of Dark Energy or any desire to give up her mission

Inspiration, so muse-like that she would inspire people to live their best, happiest life and create peace

Next, the Devils endowed GG Star with:

A mind as sharp as a knife that could think three moves ahead in challenging scenarios

A soulful charm that affected people like a drug, so that they wanted to be in her presence over and over again because people would not be able to get her out of their minds

The ability to reveal people's most secret desires, of which they were ashamed and always hiding them from others. People would look into her eyes and talk uncontrollably about everything inside their minds and hearts.

The ability to create a shield around herself in the form of a biofield that protected her against the resentment, evil, and envy of people

A spiritual companion in the form of a black cat to guard against the evil attacks and dark magic from the underworld

Despite all the gifts of the Gods and the Devils, the Planet Venus was the mother of GG Star. Mother Venus' influence was the most powerful. GG Star received from her mother an incredibly powerful sexual energy, as well as sensuality and physical sensitivity. GG Star would be able to awaken sexual desire easily and without any effort since her nature was so steeped in eroticism and magnetism. At the same time, GG Star could easily receive pleasure and enjoyment by exerting sexual influence on others. The more she used her power and the influence of sexuality, the more this power grew and the more pleasure it brought to her. The more pleasure she experienced, the more pleasure her partner experienced because her sexuality was so giving and healing to others. No one would be able to resist her superpower, even if the minds of the subjects fought against her influence. They would still succumb to her power of eroticism and desire.

Despite all her strength and power, GG Star would possess excessive elegance, grace, sophistication, and femininity. The physical body, or human shell, that Mother Venus designed in advance would harmonize all the qualities that the star possessed. Her body was very miniature, delicate, and had refined proportions. It was much smaller in size than normal female bodies. Her body was very thin and looked fragile.

GG Star's skin was softer than velvet. Her whole body was one large erogenous zone. Her face seemed innocent and pure, which added to her appeal. She was not vulgar, and outwardly exuded and spread the aura of sexuality around her in a very hormonal, natural way. An aura of sexuality exuded from her as easily as she breathed. In general, GG Star's body was an unreal work of art that Mother Venus created. It was so perfect and aesthetically pleasing that no one on Earth had a similar body.

The Sun gave GG Star a clear awareness of who she was and acted as her identity's guiding light. The Sun also gifted her with the path of creative self-expression. The Sun's gifts was why the inner compass of GG Star always guided her on the right path of personal growth and development, inspiring the desire to set goals and achieve them.

The planet Mars endowed GG Star with leadership qualities, such as courage, initiative, and the ability to fight evil. With planet Mars' gift, she could use her sexuality to fight for harmony, which made GG Star a warrior of love.

Next, planet Uranus endowed GG Star with the strength of a flexible mentality and the ability to adapt to change. She could easily adapt to a new environment, and in challenging situations, she could think quickly on her feet. The planet Uranus also gave GG Star a thirst for adventure and discovery.

The planet Pluto introduced the need for the irreversible destruction of everything old to make room for something new. With the planet Pluto's powers, GG Star would not be tied down to the past, like a chained animal. She would always strive for renewal and growth, keeping her sights focused on the future and its limitless possibilities.

The planet Saturn rewarded GG Star with a sense of self-discipline and responsibility to achieve results and material wealth. The planet Saturn made GG Star a calculated decision-maker. GG Star received the knowledge of money and power, which is exactly what was most valuable to the people of Earth in their disharmonious world overtaken by Dark Energy. In order to save the people of Earth and combat The Great Imbalance, she had to understand the allure and temptation of Dark Energy.

After that, the planet Jupiter put into GG Star a deep sense of the importance of spiritual growth. With this gift, she would know what was needed for a harmonious inner state as well as an acceptance of the world as it is. The planet Jupiter's power also instilled faith in oneself and strength into GG Star.

The planet Neptune gifted GG Star with mystery and mysticism, making her full of secrets, which added to her charm. The planet Neptune gave her the sources of feelings and impressions and formed in her a refined perception and appreciation of art. In her presence, people would be so overwhelmed with her beauty that they would very often be prone to illusions, which they happily created in their heads as if they were drunk.

Lastly, the Moon rewarded GG Star with the Soul: a deep sense of empathy, the ability to tolerate the world without condemnation or enmity, and the ability to forgive and heal. During the creation of GG Star, the Moon was waning, so the Moon deprived her of any emotional attachment to anyone or anything. GG Star would not belong to anyone, but she would exist exclusively for the mission of saving the world.

Therefore, the powerful GG Star was created, endowed with the power of the Gods and Devils, plus the gifts of the Sun, planets, and Moon. She would be a warrior of love and balance for the sake of her mission to save the world.

After they created the star, they placed it in a safe place in the galactic system, one that was shrouded in mystery and spiritual protection. She was placed in space under the protection of the planets, until the day when her soul would unite with a human body. The Gods and Devils did so because they would wait until the time was right to transfer the star's soul into a physical body, which would finalize the creation of the superhero. Only then would her superpowers become fully realized.

※

Chapter 5

A SUPERHERO IS BORN

During the general meeting of the Gods and Devils, it was decided that the child who GG Star's soul would be put into, would be born in Russia. At the child's birth, Russia was mostly isolated from the rest of the world, and it was a time of great tribulation for the Russian people. Dark Energy was strong and abundant there. The child was born into a period of chaos and unrest in Russia, which was strategic on the part of the Gods.

In such a desperate time when the Russian people were solely focused on survival, the Gods knew the child's superpowers would go unnoticed. Her father would be so exhausted from his grueling job at the factory, and her mother would be so concerned with finding more food to put on the table, that they would not notice anything supernatural about their daughter. The child's neighbors would similarly be preoccupied with the darkness of the world that even if they noticed something strange about her, they would quickly forget.

After growing not just physically and emotionally, but also in her innate cosmic gifts, the child would reach adolescence. She would observe and learn about the world and humanity from her classmates, preparing her to eventually save them. This was the cleverness of the Gods' plan. As a superhero in human form, she could better understand humanity from the ground level and best know how to rescue them from Dark Energy. When the child turned eighteen, she would finally be able to use her superpowers and become the superhero the Gods designed her to be. Her superpowers would be fully activated and ready. Then, she would be able to save the world.

As the Gods and cosmic entities planned, the soul of GG Star merged with a baby born in Siberia on May 17, 1991, at 5 a.m. She came out wailing like a banshee, announcing her presence to the world. Everyone in the hospital that day was aware of the baby born with lungs strong enough to pierce their ears with her crying. The snow of winter hadn't melted yet, but when GG Star's soul merged with the newborn baby, the snow outside her hospital window melted immediately and the ground was scorched. That was how powerful her energy force was. Siberia's harsh climate, along with the troubled social situation in Russia, hardened the child's character, like iron sharpens iron.

Her human name was Valentina. Her mother would describe her as charming, but difficult. She did not have a happy-go-lucky childhood or many fond memories. She was a demanding baby with a voracious appetite, but once she got a little older, she could take care of herself. As a child, Valentina had an unnatural maturity for her age, one that often develops when children are forced by hardship to grow up too fast.

By the time of Valentina's birth, The Great Imbalance had already swept the world. Dark energy reigned in every home, suppressing peace and harmony. Valentina's family was not immune to The Great Imbalance's effects. They were an average family of course, without anything setting them apart from the neighbors. Valentina, like all other children, grew up in an environment of strife and aggression. Tension and conflict between family members was ever present, in contrast to the unconditional love and care one would hope to raise a child with.

VALENTINA DZHERSON

In adolescence, Valentina's father lost his job at the factory and was unemployed for two years. It was a terribly difficult time for the family. Valentina's mother began taking odd jobs around the neighborhood, desperate for any way to make income to feed her family. She cleaned houses, did laundry, and sewed to scrape by with enough to buy a few loaves of bread and the ingredients for watery stew.

With her mother away, Valentina was often at home alone with her father. After he lost his job, his drinking worsened and he quickly became an alcoholic. Once alcohol took hold of him, he no longer searched for jobs or went to interviews. He would drink, watch TV, and sleep. Valentina stayed away from him and spent time in her room.

Once, he got violent with Valentina. She did something small to upset him, and in his drunken rage, he slapped her across the face. He expected her to fall back as a normal person does after being hit with such force, especially since she was a girl of about twelve years old. However, she barely budged and held her ground. When she turned her face to look at him, her father's eyes went wide in shock. Valentina slapped him back, and he went flying across the kitchen. When he came to, he had a terrible hangover and was sore all over, but couldn't remember why.

When Valentina turned fourteen, she was rapidly gaining strength and was looking for a way out. She spent less and less time at home and she spent more time at school or the local hangouts. Sometimes, she wouldn't come home at night, and instead walked the streets, observing and watching people and learning their habits. At school, her peer relationships were very difficult, but due to her super strength, Valentina never had to worry about being bullied or picked on. Her strength was no match for theirs. She had a reputation for being the arm-wrestling champion that no one, not even her gym teacher, could beat.

However, Valentina stood out among her peers, and became a source of conflict between them. All her classmates were inexplicably drawn to her, like a moth to a flame. She had that special "X factor" that made her mysterious and extraordinary. Everyone had an opinion of her, and they either loved her or hated her. No one could be indifferent to her. Disagreements about Valentina were common. She was talked and gossiped about at the lunch tables in the cafeteria and also in the teacher's lounge.

There were peers who openly and sincerely worshiped her unique charm. They became close to her and were somehow healed by her energy. They would give her gifts for no other reason than to be close to her, or have an excuse to talk to her. They longed for her to just look them in the face and lock eyes with them. Her beautiful eyes held so much intrigue and spiritual depth. These peers became kinder, more cheerful, and more confident from their proximity to Valentina. As harmony blossomed within them, they even became more sexually liberated. Unknowingly, the more time they spent in Valentina's presence, the faster their sexual awakening progressed. They became familiar with their bodies and the pleasures that came with touching themselves a certain way.

Then there were the peers who despised Valentina, jealous of her charm and sway with classmates. She was everything they wanted to be, and seeing her effortless power taunted them. These were generally older peers, and they got into fights with her, mostly to see if anyone could knock her off her pedestal. Even then in their young minds, they could detect something godlike about her. But fighting with Valentina always left them doubly hurt. They suppressed their secret admiration for her, while they put on airs of disgust. After their fights, they left bruised and beat up physically and emotionally. They felt rejected by Valentina, which further inflicted pain on them.

Valentina grew up, not only as an attractive teenager, but also one with a sharp, strong mind. Physically, she reminded boys of "Lolita," but they knew she wasn't just a pretty face. She had an intelligence that was unmatched, though she usually kept it hidden. She was not showy in class and only answered questions when the teacher called on her. Valentina was well-studied in all subjects at school, and she was easily one of the schools; brightest students. She had a sophisticated mind, a sexy body, erotic energy, and the confidence of an adult. These qualities made her attractive as hell to her classmates, and she knew it.

Valentina used her qualities to get what she wanted, and used people to reach her ends. Some people even enjoyed being used by her. She would get classmates to do small things like buy her lunch or a new article of clothing at a store. Once she grew bored of the simple tasks she could get peers to do, she wanted more of a challenge. She would convince peers to change their image, like try a new hairstyle or manner of dress. She convinced peers to break up with their boyfriends or girlfriends, and she manipulated the social dynamics of her school like a puppet master.

No one was immune from Valentina's spell, including adults. She received special privileges at school from teachers. She would arrive to school late and convince the attendance clerk to not mark her tardy or notify her parents. When she got into fights with peers because they wanted to test their strength, Valentina never got written up by the principal. In the principal's office, she would exude her natural erotic charm, which excited and frightened the principal. He knew better than to test his willpower or strength to challenge her, so he always dismissed her quickly.

Valentina had always loved teasing and seducing people. Valentina had fallen in love with that power in childhood. Holding power over people amused her, and she could manipulate their feelings, knowing exactly what needed to be done to make them feel good or bad. She experimented with and studied her power, knowing that someday she would need to use it for a bigger, more important purpose.

＊

Chapter 6

TOYING WITH CLASSMATES

S ometimes, Valentina played and manipulated the feelings of people for no particular reason, even those who sincerely loved her. She did this because she wasn't able to experience the feelings that people had for her. It just wasn't part of her nature. The Gods had not wanted her to get too attached to the humans around her, for then she might get distracted from her mission and veer off course. The best chance of pushing back against the advancing Dark Energy and reestablishing The Great Balance was Valentina, and the cosmic entities that created her could not risk any mistakes or distractions.

When Valentina was in a good mood, she was positive towards people and they were drawn to her, but as soon as her mood spoiled, she rejected everyone and isolated herself from people. She didn't even suspect how much it hurt for those who first received her approval, but then were rejected. She hadn't matured enough in her powers of reading others' emotions and inner thoughts yet. However, people willingly endured this pain because they couldn't stop loving her. Valentina's sexual power and energy was like a sweet, steaming cup of hot cocoa that people kept drinking even though it left their tongues The power of her sexual energy was simply overwhelming.

When Valentina toyed with people she earned naysayers and envious people. Valentina was so confident in herself, she didn't care who hated her. She only started noticing this negative attention when it spread to her teachers because they had authority over her. Eventually, her manipulation of peers came to the attention of her teachers, and Valentina developed a reputation as a power broker and force to be reckoned with among the student body.

For example, one spring day when Valentina was 16, it was approaching the end of the school year. It was a beautiful, warm day, which wasn't always guaranteed in Siberia, so these days were precious. There were only two weeks left of the school year, and all the students were so ready to be finished with their final exams. Valentina yearned for the freedom of summer as well, so she decided to give everyone what they wanted: a few extra days off.

Valentina knew who she needed to pull off her goal. She knew that a boy in her class loved her, even though he was dating another girl. His name was Konstantin and his girlfriend's name was Anya. Years earlier, in third grade, Konstantin tried to kiss Valentina on the playground, but she wasn't interested. He bugged her for weeks, always waiting for her and asking politely with big puppy dog eyes. Eventually, Valentina agreed to his request, but mostly in order to study human nature and see what was so special about this kiss. When she did give him a small peck on the cheek, he radiated joy, and she understood that she had a power to heal others with her radiant energy. Ever since that moment in third grade, Konstantin had been madly in love with Valentina. Even his girlfriend Anya knew it, but she pretended it wasn't true.

That spring day, Valentina slipped Konstantin a note in class. It said that if he did her a favor, she would give him another kiss, just like she did in third grade. If he accepted, he had to meet her at lunch and she would tell him what to do. She watched as he read the note and his ears went red. She felt his excitement and desire for her radiate off his body in heat waves. At lunch, he sat next to her, even though Anya was watching. Valentina told him to go into the boys bathrooms and clog all the toilets. With the toilets overflowing and bathrooms flooded, it would create chaos and the principal would have to send everyone home and cancel school the next day too in order to repair the damage. "Your wish is my command," Konstantin said breathlessly and he raced off to the bathrooms.

Everything went according to her plan. Sure enough, half an hour later, the principal came on the loudspeaker and told everyone to go home immediately. On her way out of the school building, she saw Konstantin being led by two teachers to the principal's office. Konstantin shook off their grip and ran to Valentina and asked for his kiss. In full view of teachers, classmates, and his girlfriend Anya, Valentina smirked and kissed him on the mouth. This day was the talk of the town for the next three months.

Peers were not the only victims of Valentina's games. Teachers succumbed to her influence as well. Valentina's teacher, Mrs. Morozov, hated her for the power of her sexual energy and how she could attract all the boys in her class, and even senior students too. It didn't help that Mrs. Morozov was Anya's mother, and Mrs. Morozov knew that her daughter's boyfriend, Konstantin, was in love with Valentina. Valentina's manipulation of Konstantin only added fuel to the fire of Mrs. Morozov's disdain for her.

But what infuriated the teacher most was that Valentina didn't think the class she taught, Russian, was important. Even though she was a talented student, she didn't put forth much effort in Russian class. Valentina was not bothered when she sometimes made grammatical mistakes while writing Russian. More important to her was conveying her thoughts and requests to people clearly. Perfect grammar wasn't needed if they understood exactly what she wanted them to get.

Valentina saw the teacher's hatred and therefore teased her more and more. Then, a cold war between Valentina and Mrs. Morozov began. Valentina understood everything, and the war with Mrs. Morozov complicated her everyday life at school, but it was nothing she couldn't handle. It would have been simpler

if Valentina stayed away from her Russian teacher, but Valentina's love of sexual and emotional domination was too strong. This was an opportunity too good to miss. It was like a guilty pleasure. Her love of sexual and emotional domination caused Valentina to have more and more difficulties with Mrs. Morozov. She deliberately flirted with boys in front of her Russian teacher, was late for her lessons, and sometimes deliberately did not complete her homework.

Valentina's rebellion maddened Mrs. Morozov. All the other teachers at the school were enslaved by her and so Valentina wanted Mrs. Morozov to surrender to her charm too. Some jealous girls at school who wanted her approval and to be close to her but had been rebuffed by her, united in a group against Valentina. Seeing that Mrs. Morozov was clearly opposed to Valentina, the group of girls took their Russian teacher's side, stuck up for her in class, and became teacher's pets. Sometimes they would say a snide insult or mean comment directed at Valentina, and Mrs. Morozov would let it slide or pretend not to hear. Of course, these students got high marks in Russian due to their support and loyalty to Mrs. Morozov.

The last day of Russian class, Mrs. Morozov tried to enact revenge on Valentina. She accused Valentina of cheating on the final exam. One of her enemies, who was also a teacher's pet of Mrs. Morozov, slipped a note in Valentina's desk when she got up to sharpen her pencil. The note was a study guide cheat sheet with the material on the test. Valentina saw through their ruse, but she didn't fight it. She knew that she was smarter than all of them combined, so she bided her time patiently, like an expert chess player taking their time before making their checkmate move.

After a meeting with her parents and the principal, it was decided that Valentina's punishment would be to take the exam again under close supervision, but this time the exam would be much, much harder and it would include advanced content. Valentina smiled inwardly because she had always held back in Russian class and hadn't tried her best. She knew if she tried her best and applied all her intelligence, she would easily crush the exam. Sure enough, she received a perfect score on the final exam, and Mrs. Morozov was shocked. The girl group was disappointed too because they wanted to get Valentina expelled, but their plan failed.

Valentina was not at all bothered by the girl group. As she could read people's inner desires, she knew they secretly admired her and were very jealous of her beauty, charm, intelligence, and strength. The girls were not confident in themselves and therefore lashed out at those who were. Valentina was not worried about coexisting with a group of enemies, since the inner harmony she was born with kept her in a state of constant balance.

Moreover, since Valentina was born at a time of chaos and Dark Energy in the country, she grew up in a family where conflicts provoked by her father were normal. She was accustomed to conflict and interpersonal strife. For Valentina, this model of behavior was familiar from childhood. Because Valentina was still only a teenager, her father and Mrs. Morozov had authority over her. While they had authority over her in position only, she held sway over them in reality through her sexual power and cosmic strength.

Conflicts based on people's hidden sexual desires in school and at home became more common. People were so animalistically attracted to her, that it sometimes frightened them and they hid their desires or suppressed them. By suppressing those strong sexual desires for so long, eventually they would erupt like a volcano and act out of jealousy. It did not help that Valentina's sexual power grew every year and became less and less controllable. Sometimes it healed people, and sometimes it hurt people.

All of Valentina's enemies were people who were secretly in love with her and had a huge sexual desire for her, which they hid and suppressed within themselves, masking their true desires with aggression. Gradually, her enemies' suppressed feelings of desire caved under the pressure of aggression towards her, and their feelings transformed into huge resentment, hatred, and anger.

Valentina paid her enemies no mind. She knew they were destined for more hardship anyway because the feeling of hatred filled the hearts of people from the inside and destroyed them. These people would begin to energetically weaken and hurt, and their sexual energy would leave them. Sexuality is life, and sexuality is health. By losing sexual energy, people no longer could live and enjoy life, only merely exist sadly. Thus, all of Valentina's haters destroyed themselves and were rendered harmless.

Throughout her childhood and teenage years, Valentina's sexual power grew, developed, and intensified. Each day that went by, she became more and more powerful, and those around her took notice. As was planned by the Gods and Devils at her creation, Valentina's sexual superpower had to be activated at the age of 18, by nature of Mother Venus. On her eighteenth birthday, after she left her hometown and went to the city of Tomsk to study at the university, Valentina's superpowers were fully activated and her journey as a superhero truly began.

※

Chapter 7

A SUPERHERO EPIPHANY

It happened at 5 am.

Valentina had only found an apartment a few days before, and she was still settling into her new life in Tomsk. Now that she mostly found the furniture she needed for her apartment, she would go looking for jobs soon. She had been tired from moving and so far was having a deep, restful sleep.

While Valentina was still sleeping in bed, she had a dream that would change her life trajectory forever. This dream would awaken her superpowers and start her superhero journey. She had a dream in which she saw her entire transformation into a superhero and the whole story of her creation by the Gods, Devils, Planets, Sun, and Moon.

In the dream, Valentina stood on an invisible floor with only the blackest of black around her. Slowly, she saw a light blink on in the distance, and Valentina realized it was a star. She watched, transfixed at the star, as it grew larger and brighter. Valentina couldn't tell if she was moving towards the star, or the star was advancing to her. Either way, it was the most beautiful thing she had ever seen. The star burned brightly and consisted of a gorgeous collection of purple, pink, and yellow colors.

Even though Valentina did not remember ever seeing this star, it somehow felt familiar to her. She felt a deep sense of kinship with it. Even as it got closer and closer, she was not afraid. She knew it wouldn't harm her. Suddenly, the star was right in front of her, and it was the size of a house. Valentina couldn't look away at its brilliance. The colors and energy spun around the star as it floated in front of her. Then, Valentina heard a voice that broke the silence.

"Valentina, this is your mother," the voice said. It was both loud and commanding, but also as soft as a whisper in her ear. "I am Planet Venus, but to you I am Mother Venus, and I am your true mother. The star you see before you is a mirror."

"What do you mean, a mirror?" Valentina said, stepping closer to the giant star before her.

"You're looking at yourself," Mother Venus replied. "The star is you, and you are not Valentina. You are GG Star."

Valentina reached out her hand and touched the star. It felt hot, but her hand didn't burn. The heat drew her in and all of sudden, she was pulled inside the star. It felt like slipping into a warm bath. No longer was Valentina in her human shell. She had become one with her true form. No longer was she Valentina, but she was now GG Star.

"You were created by the Gods, Devils, Planets, Sun, and Moon, and all the cosmic entities of the universe," Mother Venus said. As she spoke, GG Star zoomed throughout the universe and witnessed the events as Mother Venus described them. She saw the meeting of the Gods and Devils, plus the moment of her creation. "We created a star and poured all our gifts and powers into it, into you. While each cosmic entity left its fingerprint on your design, you were made most in my image, and I had the greatest influence on you."

"What powers did you give me?" GG Star asked. She now saw the Planet Venus up close, and its milky white and orange surface gleamed. She was drawn to its magnetism, and she could feel a maternal presence emanating from it. She knew without a doubt that the Planet Venus was indeed her mother. They were made of the same powers, and they attracted each other like magnets.

"GG Star, from me, you received an incredibly powerful sexual energy, as well as sensuality and physical sensitivity. You are able to awaken sexual desire easily in humans and without any effort since your nature is so steeped in eroticism and magnetism. You've noticed this already, haven't you? You've already used this power on humans to accomplish your goals."

"Yes, I have," GG Star said, thinking back to all the classmates and teachers she manipulated and toyed with during her childhood and teenage years. "But how am I living among humans if I am a star?"

"Since you were born as GG Star, your physical star will always be in space, under the care of all the other cosmic entities. But your soul lives in a human body. We transferred your star soul into a human baby, so you could live among humans on Earth. Plus, your star soul transferred all the cosmic entities' magical abilities and superpowers into the body you occupy as a shell. So even though you live in a human shell, you still have all your divine powers."

"But what is my purpose? Why did you create me?" GG Star asked. She now looked at Earth, as it spun with its blue and green colors. The small white moon orbited it slowly.

Mother Venus told GG Star about her super mission of saving the world. This was the goal of the dream, so she could not only know who she was but what she was created to accomplish. Mother Venus explained how the proliferation and expansion of Dark Energy led to The Great Imbalance, which was destroying the Earth and making all its people miserable. She told GG Star about every single one of her powers and gifts, so she was aware of her full arsenal. She would need each one of these powers to

win this difficult battle against Dark Energy and the forces that wanted to see it take over the Earth.

"GG Star, I have advice for you. Your sexual superpower is so great that you, need to periodically let it out because otherwise this power will begin to influence and control not only the people around you but also you!" Mother Venus' voice echoed in GG Star's ears. "The entire Planet Earth is in danger and only GG Star with high sexual energy can save it, so you must not fail us. Dark Energy has overwhelmed the souls and hearts of people. They live unhappily in their sad lives full of disharmony and anxiety. Only you, GG Star, can return their vitality, inspiration, and inner harmony through your sexuality."

"I accept my mission, Mother Venus," GG Star responded. She felt invigorated with the clarity of her life purpose. It felt like all the pieces of her life finally fit together, and she could step back and see its final image. She knew what she had to do. It was a monumental challenge and mission before her, but GG Star knew that she had what it would take to accomplish it and make her Mother Venus proud. If she was the only one to restore balance in the universe, then so be it. She was ready.

"Also, since you are not human, but only existing in a human shell in which the soul of a super star lives, you can never have any kind of close relationship with a human," Mother Venus said. "You are much stronger than humans, and they will see an escape from their pathetic lives in your presence. While that is indeed your mission, you must be careful because every human will want to get as close as possible to you. You must set boundaries with them.

"I understand," GG Star said. She thought back to her life in Siberia and realized that was how she had been living already. She interacted with people, but never got close to them. It came natural for her to have this distance.

"This is why from now on, I will give you a best friend and helper, who is going to protect you from black magic and negative forces of the Underworld. Your helper will be a black cat who will follow and watch over you everywhere. I will come to you again in your dreams if you need another message or guidance. Until then, goodbye GG Star, and good luck with your mission."

GG Star felt herself being drawn out of the star and back into human form. She was Valentina again, standing as a human in front of the giant, glowing star. It slowly moved away from her until it got smaller and smaller, then disappeared into the distance. She was back again, standing on the invisible floor in pitch black darkness.

Valentina opened her eyes and felt that her body was filled with strong energy. Her hands vibrated and pulsated with an immense power that came from within her. She could feel her sexual power coursing through her veins. Valentina's skin became extremely sensitive across her entire body. This was a skill that would become very useful when seducing others and manipulating them to do her bidding.

Valentina also found a purring black kitten at her feet on top of the bed. She took it in her arms and pet it softly. She would name it Patrul, which meant "patrol" in Russian, since it would be keeping watch over her and patrolling her surroundings for any evil magic. The cat purred happily, but Valentina could also sense its mystical powers, and she knew it was far from an ordinary pet.

Valentina remembered her colorful dream exactly, to the smallest detail. While it was an unexpected turn of events, she was not particularly surprised by the story Mother Venus told her since this was the only logical explanation for her natural power of beauty and charm. Huge sexual potential overwhelmed her body and asked for a way out. After all, in this way, through the release of the surplus of her sexual potential, she was able to help people, which was her nature and mission. She couldn't wait to begin exercising her powers for her mission.

The only things that united her with people was her human body and name, while all her essence and power were cosmic and divine. However, to save the world, Valentina needed to live among people. Subconsciously, she had always known that she was more than just human, and she did her best to fit in as much as her powers allowed. Now that she knew about her true nature, she would have to keep her origin and history secret.

Valentina realized and understood who she was and why she was on this earth. The next step was to find a method of influencing the masses with her strong sexual energy, so she could awaken their inspiration, joy of life, passion, and strong emotions. She would do this all for the sake of restoring inner harmony in society as a whole as well as restoring order to the universe, so The Great Balance could once again govern the universe. Valentina did not know exactly what to do, but she was sure that the stars would give her some kind of sign.

※

PART 3

GG Star's Mission

※

Chapter 8

VALENTINA'S WEBCAM DEBUT

After a few weeks, Valentina was settling into her new life in Tomsk. She had furnished her apartment, purchased school supplies, and registered for her university classes. It had been more difficult finding a job than she expected, so she decided to put it off until her university classes began.

Valentina thought that being a university student would be a good opportunity to meet many new kinds of people. It would help her mission of understanding humans, so she could save them. When she was a student in childhood, she learned about the ways of adolescents and teenagers, but now was the time for her to learn about the world of adults and their heartaches, passions, loneliness, and insecurities. She would continue to live her normal human life, despite her superhero status, until she figured out a clear plan to fulfill her mission. Like any good soldier, she needed to get a lay of the land first before planning her attack.

VALENTINA DZHERSON

On the first day of university, Valentina picked up her purse filled with her school supplies and locked her apartment. As soon as she appeared on the street, everyone outside began to turn around and look at her. They all felt an unexplainable yearning for her. Both men and women felt this magnetic pull towards Valentina. No one could be indifferent to her presence. These people even wondered, "Is this love at first sight?" But before anyone could approach her, Valentina hurried to the bus stop. Even though she sensed the emptiness in each of their hearts and she had ideas of how to heal them, there was no way Valentina would be late for her first day of university, so she brushed off these thoughts.

Valentina waited for the traffic light to change, so she could cross the street and reach the bus stop. As she turned to glance at the traffic light, she suddenly noticed an advertisement stapled to the telephone pole next to her. The advertisement read: "URGENT! In need of a webcam model. Call the phone number below!" Curious, Valentina tore off a slip with the phone number, but before she could think any more of it, the traffic light changed. She stuffed the slip into her coat pocket and hurried across the street to catch the bus.

In her first university class, Valentina caused a scene, which was not her intention. It happened twice in fact. First, while the professor was calling the role, he glanced up when she said her name. He was a middle-aged man who was balding and a bit fat. There was something alluring and sensual about her voice that made the professor want to see what this student looked like. When the professor saw Valentina in all her amazing beauty, he dropped his coffee mug, and it shattered on the classroom floor, spilling hot coffee everywhere. The professor went red in the face and apologized for his accident. Of course, this incident drew even more attention to Valentina from her classmates because they wanted to see the girl who made the professor drop his coffee.

The second time Valentina caused a scene was in her final class of the day. This professor was an old woman with long, gray hair. She was fashionable and she had aged well. Valentina could tell the professor was doing her best not to look at her in the crowd of students. Valentina, using her powers of perception and reading human's hearts, detected that this professor was secretly bisexual, but due to the conservative university, had kept her sexuality under wraps. This commotion was not caused by the professor, however. This one was caused by the students. When the professor told the class that they needed to choose a partner for the semester-long project, students flooded toward Valentina, asking if she would be their partner. She politely declined all their offers and instead chose to partner with a shy boy named Pavel in the back of the auditorium. She sensed that Pavel needed a confidence boost, and his demeanor glowed when she spoke to him.

After her first day at university, Valentina was an extremely popular girl, and everyone wanted her. She wanted to test her strength and its impact on people, so she agreed to let the best guys and the most beautiful girls come closer to her. She didn't have to make a lot of effort. All she had to do was just touch them with her hand and look into their eyes with passion and tenderness as they turned into madmen in love. Her touch and eye contact were intoxicating, almost like a drug overdose. People felt that they were overly in love with Valentina and their hearts nearly burst. This love made them suffer. They were obsessed with her and worshiped her like slaves.

Valentina realized quickly that she could not influence each person with her power personally when meeting, as it would take too long to heal the whole world one by one. It had taken working as Pavel's partner for three whole weeks before he began to reach a harmonious state with healthy confidence and self-esteem. Secondly, with her influence, this force could have an overdose effect and destroy a person. Valentina realized that soon Pavel was swinging to the opposite extreme, so confident and self-assured that he was egotistical and vain. His vanity made him approach beautiful women at bars and hit on them, even with their muscular boyfriends at their sides. Pavel got beat up several times before Valentina asked her professor for a new partner because her power was influencing him too much. Pavel was receiving too high of a dose of her healing power, so Valentina cut him off.

One night after she had finished her schoolwork and fed Patrul, Valentina's landlord knocked on the door and told her he needed her rent for the month. Valentina went into her bedroom where she kept her stash of money and realized that her savings was quickly dwindling. After a month of living in Tomsk and at-

tending university classes, she really needed to find a job and get a regular source of income. She paid the landlord and sat down, petting Patrul and wondering where she could find a good job.

At this moment, Valentina remembered the announcement for a webcam model that she found on the first day of university classes. She went through her coat pockets and found the slip of paper with the phone number. Valentina did not really know what a webcam model was and how it worked, but she had a strong feeling that she should try it and see how it fit her. She decided to call the number to find out more about the job. A gruff man answered the phone and said his name was Ivan, the studio manager.

"What kind of job are you looking for?" Ivan asked her.

"A job that pays money," Valentina said with a laugh, and Ivan laughed with her. He sounded gruff, but her charm softened his tone and he grew a liking for her.

"If you do the job right, you can make a lot of money at our studio," he said.

They talked more about the job details and Ivan invited her to the studio for a test run.

"Normally, we have a formal interview and see what you would be like as a webcam model, but I think you can skip that part. I can tell you have an attractive personality that people will be drawn to. Plus, if your body is half as attractive as your voice, you'll be very popular," Ivan said. "How about you come to the studio tomorrow for a test run and see how it goes?"

"That sounds great. I'll see you tomorrow. Oh Ivan, should I wear any special outfit?" Valentina asked.

"Bring something sexy," he said.

The next day, Valentina decided to skip her university classes to go to the studio. She was an extremely bright student, so it wouldn't matter if she missed a class. She could always seduce a fellow classmate to give her the notes she missed anyway. Valentina wore a simple dress, but underneath, she was wearing sexy black lingerie.

When she arrived at the address Ivan had given her on the phone, the studio looked like a big apartment with many rooms. Each room had a sofa and a computer with a webcam, and each room had some girls who worked there behind a closed door. Even the kitchen was occupied and used as a working space. After a woman gave her a tour of the studio, she told Valentina to wait for Ivan to come and talk with her.

A few minutes later, Ivan came in and greeted her. He was a burly, hairy man who looked like a bouncer at a nightclub. His body was intimidating to a normal person, but his personality was kind and gentle. Ivan was a bit shocked when he saw how young-looking Valentina was. He did not believe she was 18 years old because she had such a baby face and an extra skinny body. He checked her ID to make sure she was in fact of legal age, but he still was not sure that the studio was a good place for her.

"Do you still not believe I'm 18?" Valentina asked him.

"No, of course I believe you now. I can see it on your ID. I'm not sure you're a good fit with our studio. You see, you look so innocent and pure. Most of our webcam models look their age. We've never had a model look so young," Ivan said.

"Doesn't that make me an asset?" Valentina asked. "I'll stand out as a different model that will grab the viewers' attention. They've never seen anyone like me before."

"Maybe. I know I sounded confident about you fitting in when we spoke on the phone, but now I'm not so sure," Ivan said.

Judging from his body language, heart rate, and inner desires, Valentina knew that most of Ivan's uncertainty about her working there was because he was insanely attracted to her personally. Ivan tried his best not to hire webcam models who he was extremely attracted to because it made things complicated for him at work. At the end of the day, he had a job to do. He had to run the studio and he didn't want to constantly fight temptation every time he supervised a model he yearned for.

"It's time to use your powers to convince him," Valentina thought to herself.

"Do you have any tissues?" Valentina asked, pretending to get emotional. She made her eyes water. "I just need a job so bad, and I'm afraid I'll be kicked out of my apartment if I don't start making money soon."

Ivan handed her a box of tissues and she purposely dropped it. He went to get it, but Valentina stopped him.

"Don't worry, I'll get it," she said, then she seductively bent over in front of Ivan. She made her dress hike up in the back, exposing her ass and the sexy black lingerie she was wearing. Out of the corner of her eye, she saw Ivan stiffen and his eyes go wide at her body. Valentina knew that Ivan would cave to her demands. After a few more minutes of talking, she used her strong mind, attitude, and magical power of sexuality to make him give her a chance to try out being a webcam model.

Ivan showed Valentina to a free room and very quickly explained to her how the webcam business worked and all the rules.

"Now that you know how to operate the computer, you should be good to go. I'll be watching your webcam to evaluate your performance, then we'll talk about how the test run went and if you got the job," Ivan said, shutting the door behind him.

"He's in for the performance of his lifetime," Valentina thought to herself with a smirk.

※

Chapter 9

RISE TO FAME

The webcam performance was the perfect place for Valentina to realize herself and release all her sexy power as GG Star. She directed this strong energy to a huge number of people from all over the world at the same time. The effect was magical. When viewers saw the new girl, they immediately recognized that something about her was different. She had that "x factor" that not many webcam performers had. The power of her sexuality attracted everyone to her chat. Within a few minutes, her chat room was filled with hundreds of viewers. People just admired her, and as Valentina started to show off her sexy lingerie to the camera, her computer pinged with tips. In fact, the computer almost pinged non-stop because viewers spoiled her with tips. They threw money at her, so grateful to just be in her presence even if it was only online.

GG Star then took off the top of her lingerie, exposing her breasts. The chat went wild. She was worshiped as a goddess for her natural performance ability. People could not stop watching her, and their eyes were glued to the screen as she seductively danced to the music and touched herself. As the viewers watched her, they felt blessed. They also felt relief from their sadness, loneliness, and any negativity that was bringing them down.

The more GG Star performed and shared her sexual power, the more powerful she became. People were happy to give her money for the emotional healing that they got from her. The more people she healed, the richer GG Star became. The viewers knew the immense value of the performance and healing they were experiencing. There was no price too high for such joy and relief, and people had to pay for their own therapy if they wanted to invest in themselves.

GG Star eventually took off the rest of her black lingerie and performed naked. When she was online, people were mesmerized by her charm and the sincerity of her performance. They saw natural pleasure in her face and body movements. She did not play or act like it was rehearsed. She honestly demonstrated the whole palette of her own emotions and feelings, and as she shared her sexuality, it revived people's souls and unthawed their hearts. GG Star openly showed the whole essence of her nature and character. She was authentic in her performance and communication with people. This is why people fell in love with her and were able to feel love within themselves again. She was an example of embracing your sexual power, celebrating pleasure, and indulging in what felt good.

GG Star was filled with the power of the Gods and the magic of the planets. All of the cosmos existed within her. It was impossible to ignore her vitality and the magic she embodied. She exuded the healing power of sexuality and directed it to the people watching her, which brought their emotions back to life. They sincerely fell in love with her, found love again within themselves, and felt harmony in their souls. She could feel the Dark Energy within them disappearing and Light Energy taking home in their souls once more.

Watching GG Star and her sincere sexual performance, they again felt like happy people and began to show interest in life and living it to the fullest. They found harmony in their souls through

sexual and spiritual arousal. She possessed such strength that she was able to induce an erection even in impotent men. During her performance, viewers became satisfied and kind, they believed in themselves, and they wanted to live. For them, GG Star was a motivator for success, an icon of sexuality, and an example of personal freedom. She was a masterpiece that showcased the result of being themselves! By her example, GG Star positively influenced people, affirming the need to maintain their individuality, listen to their true sexual desires, and satisfy them.

After finishing her first webcam session, Ivan came into her room and couldn't stop talking about how incredible her debut performance was. He was in shock. In fact, he stopped the performances of the other webcam girls and had them watch Valentina's performance with him. He wanted them to learn from her. Ivan counted the tips she made and told her the amount of her payout from this two-hour performance. It was a lot of money. Valentina really loved money, as it was a symbol of power and infinite possibilities. She was very glad to see how many people she made happy and that they showed their appreciation for her show and emotional-sexual therapy. In this case, it was a double win: people received both joy and healing treatment, while GG Star got really good money and made a great living.

After Valentina said goodbye to Ivan, she left the studio and started walking home. It was a dark night. The bank was closed, so she would have to go tomorrow morning to open a checking and savings account. That way Ivan could send all the money she earned during her webcam performances into her bank account. The bank teller would be surprised if they knew how much money Valentina made in only two hours.

Valentina decided to walk home instead of taking the bus. She was still fairly new to Tomsk and wanted to explore this part of the city. Little did she know, this area of the city wasn't the safest at night. Normally, Valentina's extremely perceptive mind would have picked up on this fact easily, due to the abandoned storefronts and shady figures lurking in the shadows of the streets. However, Valentina was too distracted by her immensely successful webcam debut. She had never felt so powerful before. She wooed and seduced many people before of course, but to have an audience of so many people watching and adoring her all at once was another level of power. Thinking back to that webcam experience made her tipsy, as if she had been drinking alcohol.

"Hey sweetie," a voice called out to her from the darkness of a nearby alley. "Can you help me with something?"

Valentina looked over and saw who was speaking. It was a dirty-looking man in a beat-up coat. It looked like he hadn't showered in a few days. His hair was disheveled and he had a scraggly beard.

"He must be homeless," Valentina thought to herself. "My mission is to help save the world, so I should help him too, shouldn't I? It would be wrong of me to discriminate and not help the homeless."

While this certainly was true, Valentina should've known that it was a trap. If she hadn't been feeling tipsy off her webcam performance, she would've noticed the two other men hiding in the shadows behind the dumpster.

"What do you need help with, sir?" Valentina said as she walked into the alley.

"He needs somebody to warm him up, sweetie," a big man said to her left. He looked as tall as a giant and had burly arms and a unibrow. He gave her a grin, and Valentina saw he had two gold teeth. He held a wooden bat in his meaty hand.

"In fact, we all could use a warm body to lay next to. You sure do fit the bill," a small man said to her right. He emerged from behind the dumpster, and Valentina saw that even though he was scrawny, he had a sharp knife in his hand.

Valentina finally realized that she was in danger as the three men surrounded her with evil intentions. These kinds of men were the result of The Great Imbalance. Dark Energy poured out of them and swirled inside their souls. They had nothing to live for, so they preyed on women to satisfy their terrible desires. She could see the lust and violence in their hearts, and she knew she needed to act fast to diffuse the situation.

"No problem," Valentina thought. "I'll just use my powers to seduce them and bend them to my will. Before long, they'll be begging at my feet, and they'll do anything I tell them to, including getting as far away from me as possible."

Valentina opened up her coat to show them her black lingerie. The men gasped in awe of her beauty, and their desires for her only intensified.

"I can help you, but you gentlemen need to help me first," Valentina said seductively. "I dropped my ring in this alley yesterday. Go find it for me in all this mess," she lied. Once the men were busy looking in all the trash, she could make her escape.

"We ain't got time for all that," the big giant of a man said, grabbing Valentina's arm.

Shocked that her powers weren't working on them, Valentina concentrated harder and looked the men straight in the eyes. But the men paid no attention to her because their eyes were focused on her amazing body. She couldn't make eye contact with them to use her powers. The first man with disheveled hair put a dirty hand on Valentina's leg, and when she tried to squirm away, the scrawny man held his knife up to her throat.

"Get off me," Valentina said, trying in vain to get away. The burly giant started kissing her neck, and she started to panic.

Suddenly, something hissed behind Valentina. She turned and saw her black cat Patrul with his hair raised in anger and his yellow eyes glaring at the men.

"Get that cat out of here. Slice it if you have to," the first man said to the scrawny one with the knife.

But when the scrawny man went to kick the cat, Patrul transformed into a creature ten times larger than an ordinary house cat. In a second, Patrul had turned into a black panther! Patrul made a deep, guttural snarl that made even the hairs raise on Valentina's neck, and she knew that she was in no danger.

Patrul pounced on the scrawny man, biting his hand and knocking the knife from his grasp. Patrul bared his sharp teeth to the other two men, and they let go of Valentina immediately.

"What the hell? Let's get out of here," the burly giant yelled, his voice quivering with fear. He grabbed the scrawny man, and the three of them ran as fast as they could into the street and away from the large cat.

Valentina caught her breath, as Patrul transformed back into a regular black cat. She knelt down to pet him.

"Oh Patrul, thank goodness you saved me," she said. "I don't know what happened, but my powers weren't working on them."

Patrul looked at her and communicated with her telepathically, which he had never done before.

"Your energy is depleted, which has weakened your powers and sexual power," Patrul's voice said in her mind. "You were also cocky and arrogant from feeling so strong, which clouded your judgment. Even though you are a superhero and you have cosmic superpowers, it doesn't mean you're without weakness. You need to be wiser and more alert next time. You're still learning your powers, and the more you practice, the stronger and wiser you'll be. You'll know your limits and when to conserve energy, so you're not found in a weak position like you were tonight."

"How did you know I was in danger?" she asked. "You followed me?"

"I'm always nearby, watching over you, whether you see me or not," Patrul said.

"My webcam performance must have taken up a lot of my energy," Valentina said. "Using my powers on so many people at once was more taxing than I thought. You're right. I'll be wiser and more careful from now on. Thanks, Patrul."

Later that night, as she washed her body in a hot shower, Valentina reflected on the day. It had been an exciting and eventful day, full of new experiences and new lessons. Unfortunately, it had included danger too, but luckily Mother Venus had sent Patrul to watch over her. She didn't want to rely on him to always protect her. She had to be ready to use her superpowers to protect herself.

"Despite my mistake, today felt like a big step in the right direction of my mission," Valentina thought as she massaged shampoo into her hair. *"I learned that I can help and heal lots of people at once through my webcam performances. It's more efficient than only working on one person at a time, which is what I have been doing. I'm going to keep doing the webcam performances and see where it leads me."*

※

Chapter 10

LIFE AS A SEXY LIBRARIAN

The next morning, Valentina went to university like usual. She woke up fully refreshed and recharged, so her superpowers were back to full strength. Since last night's webcam performance and all the people she healed and all the money she made, Valentina beamed with confidence. Her superpower of sensuality was fully on, and therefore she was too much for people. They couldn't be so close to her. People felt the superpower radiating off of her, and they gave her space on the street and kept their distance. It was like they were looking directly into the sun and had to shield their eyes.

When Valentina entered the university classroom, it was the same. Normally, her classmates fought over who could sit next to her in the auditorium, especially the male students who she toyed with and seduced. After a month into the school year, she had hooked up with nearly all of them in her class in one way or another. They would invite her to their dorm room for a study session, or to the library's shelves to look for textbooks together. Inevitably, it would end up with them having sex--that is, if Valen-

tina wanted it. Most of the times she did, but sometimes she didn't feel like it, or she wanted to deny them sex to manipulate and toy with them, making them yearn for it all the more. However, today in her Sociology class, her powers were so strong that there were empty seats all around her in the auditorium.

Anyone who got too close to Valentina got burned or hurt. This happened because the male classmates, and even some female ones, put a lot of expectations on her to return their love and adoration, but Valentina just enjoyed flirting. Of course, no one knew that she was not like all other young women her age and that she didn't have any emotional attachment in her nature at all. She enjoyed sex and sexual communication, but sometimes she would just leave without saying goodbye. She didn't even know this could hurt people, as she didn't feel anything.

Little did she know that she had hurt one of her classmates the night before when she was doing her webcam performance. His name was Stepan and he was in her Sociology class. He had begged her for a week to come to his birthday party. Earlier in the week, Stepan asked her again if she would come. He wanted her to meet his friends. He had told them all about her. Valentina told him that she would go to his birthday party if he did a dare. The dare was to go into the men's bathroom, strip of all his clothes, and wait for her to come in so they could have sex.

"What do you mean?" Stepan said with wide eyes. Valentina detected a quickened pulse and increased productions of saliva in his mouth, both signs of sexual arousal. She knew he had always wanted her, but had been too afraid of rejection to ask. She also knew that he was planning on kissing her or making a move at his birthday party.

"I mean what I said. If you want me to go to your party, go in that bathroom over there," she said, pointing to the men's bathroom outside of the classroom, "get naked, and knock twice when you're ready. Then I'll come in and we'll have sex. Isn't that what you've always wanted?"

Stepan bit his lip and nodded vigorously, then raced into the bathroom. He had to wait for one man to leave the bathroom before he could do what she commanded.

"I can't believe this is actually happening," Stepan thought as he took off his clothes. *"Not only is she also attracted to me physically, but I think she likes me too! She's going to come to my birthday party, and all my friends will finally see how hot she is. They've been teasing me, saying that I made her up. Maybe the party will be the start of our relationship."*

They had sex in the bathroom, and it was the best Stepan had ever had. Their moans echoed in the bathroom so everyone in the hallways could hear them, but no one said a thing because they didn't want to stop what sounded like pure ecstasy.

The night of Stepan's birthday party was last night, when Valentina decided to give webcam performing a try. She had forgotten about the party entirely. When Stepan saw her in Sociology class this morning, he was so distraught and upset with her for not showing up.

"You said you would come to my birthday party. Everyone expected you. I was so embarrassed," Stepan said.

"I forgot about it," Valentina said with a shrug before turning back to the professor's lecture. "What was the party for anyway? Can't you just throw another one?"

"You're heartless. I can't believe it. You're as cold as ice," Stepan said.

"Of course I have a heart. I'm alive, aren't I? Didn't you feel my heart beating against yours when we were on top of each other in the bathroom a few days ago?" Valentina asked. Stepan stormed out of the auditorium crying.

Valentina didn't understand what Stepan meant and why he told her she was heartless. She was accustomed to people creating drama and becoming so hysterical just because she was not hopelessly in love with them. Valentina sincerely could not understand why people couldn't embrace the feeling of lust and attraction they felt because of her. They always had to ruin it because they wanted something deeper, but she couldn't be tied down to one person like that. Valentina had never been in a relationship, and she didn't care to be. She never felt like she needed it, and romance didn't interest her.

When she was eating lunch later that day, she thought about all the drama with her male classmates. University was a good idea at first, but maybe she had outgrown it. She knew all she needed to know about adult humans, plus since she was so smart, she didn't need to learn any subject taught by the university. In reality, she could be teaching the professors. She didn't really need a university degree, and her mission was to massively spread the healing power of sexual energy and save the world from the influence of Dark Energy. She was tasked with restoring The Great Balance and creating peace and harmony inside each and every person on Earth. There was no university class about that. Valentina decided all the hassle of navigating her relationships with her classmates wasn't worth it. She was sick of people getting hurt and crying out for her to love them. Valentina decided to quit university and focus on her new job as a webcam performer instead. However, that was only in the evenings, so she would need something to do during the day.

Valentina was a very intelligent person and easily got a job at the best library in the city. It was a quiet place, and during her free time from visitors, Valentina loved to read. She knew exactly where each book was located and could quickly find them on the shelves. Since she did not really want to socialize with people, as it was not her goal and because she didn't have much in common with them, she felt quite comfortable in the library. It was nice to have Patrul with her too and the black cat walked with her everywhere.

In the human world, it was necessary to have a spiritual guardian like Patrul watch over her since many people, due to the influence of Dark Energy, were filled with envy and anger. These people could easily wish each other evil, including Valentina, which is why Patrul's presence was important. Of course, Valentina was not quite a human, but she was still vulnerable to Dark Magic.

Since she had a perfect body, she was an easy target for haters. To avoid the slightest chance of the evil eye or damage caused by people's envy or anger, Patrul defended her like a talisman.

When people met Valentina, they considered her a unique anomaly. She had proud posture, perfect body proportions, and a rare thinness with beautiful toned muscles. She was small, but at the same time had long legs, very narrow hips and a firm, round ass. She had naturally highlighted hair, which many women would've killed for because they spend hundreds of dollars a month getting their hair colored to look like hers. Valentina had beautiful skin, and absolutely no makeup was needed since her natural beauty was authentic. Looking at her from the back, library guests saw a teenager, and when they looked into her face, they saw a charming angel. However, if they were lucky enough to talk to her, people found out that she had a devilishly sharp and strong mind.

As an employee at the library, Valentina was always in high spirits and felt quite satisfied with herself. She had no complexes of incompleteness or imposter syndrome. She knew how to live in the present moment, not remaining in the past or rushing into the future. Simply put, there was no one like Valentina.

Of course, Valentina always looked great at work. Usually, she dressed in various very short, tight-fitting dresses that accentuated her sophisticated figure and grace. She also wore high heels, and she had hair neatly gathered in a ponytail that seductively fell over her right shoulder. As an accessory, Valentina loved various women's backpacks as it was convenient to carry a cat in them. Patrul rode with her on the way to work in her backpack, and then she would let him out to roam and follow her in the library. She also loved to use a perfume that filled the space of the library in a subtle but sexy way.

Everyone who visited the library, even just once, was always a bit in love with Valentina, and she stuck in their minds days after their visit. Visitors, no matter their gender or age, always flirted with her. They strangely felt free to talk about anything with her, including very personal stuff. Somehow the conversations always led to them confessing and disclosing their own deepest desires to her. Visitors told her secret things that they had never told anyone before. Valentina always gave them the books they asked for, but she would also sneak in a book or two that she recommended for them. After listening to their secret confessions, she would find a book that would help them realize their inner desires and become more comfortable with the pleasure they sought. To offer people even more powerful healing, Valentina put the address of her webcam website on their book slip. That way, they knew where she did her sexy, healing performances via the webcam streaming as GG Star. In this way, Valentina helped people during the day as a sexy librarian and also in the evening as a webcam performer.

✳

Chapter 11

THE PAINTER

One day, a young man, who was about 35 years old, came to the library. He was a thin man with curly hair and a mustache. He was handsome in an ordinary way, and he dressed fashionably and wore a black turtleneck. Valentina could tell he was an artist just by looking at him. There was something creative about him. She stood behind the library desk and scanned in returned books with Patrul at her side.

"Excuse me, can you help me?" the man asked. He looked discouraged and downcast, like he was having more than just a bad day, but a bad week or month. "I need help looking for a book. I was hoping you could make a recommendation for me."

"Of course, I'll be happy to help you," Valentina said, sensing the Dark Energy that was weighing down his soul. "What kind of book are you looking for?"

"I need a book that will help increase my creative power as an artist. I'm a painter, you see, and I have a big project to finish," he said. "A rich family paid me a large commission fee to paint a mural in a room in their mansion. It's a very important location because the room is where they host social events and balls. Their guests are very influential, and some are wealthy politicians or royalty from other countries. The mural has to be fantastic. It has to speak to every soul who sees it. The mural has to be more than just beautiful. It has to transcend beauty and somehow give people comfort and peace in their hearts."

Valentina glanced at Patrul with a smile. The painter was describing her exact mission: to restore The Great Balance of Light and Dark Energy in order to bring peace, harmony, and love to the world. The painter had no idea that Valentina was the perfect person to talk to about his problem. She was actually the most perfect person on Earth to discuss his problem with, and she was the best person on Earth to help him. Not only could she help this one man, but if he painted a mural inspired by Light Energy, the rich family and all their guests would be healed too.

"I see," Valentina said in an understanding and gentle tone. "It sounds like a big task indeed. I agree that you'll definitely need all the creative power you have within you to accomplish it. But, you're looking for more than just a creativity boost, aren't you? I sense that there's something else that's holding you back. Am I correct?"

The painter looked shy and averted Valentina's knowing gaze, but he nodded in agreement. She could see right into his heart, and while she knew what was going on, she had to pretend she didn't and let him explain it to her. Having the painter talk through his problem was an important part of his healing process.

"Is there somewhere more private we can talk?" he asked, glancing around at the other library patrons who were perusing the bookshelves. No one seemed to be paying much attention to them, but they were within earshot and could easily eavesdrop if they wanted to.

Valentina nodded and led him to a quiet corner of the library. There was a reading room in the back that most people didn't know about. They sat down and the painter told Valentina more about what was really going on with him.

"This is the biggest project I've ever been commissioned to complete, and I'm nervous. I worry that I'm not able to live up to their expectations. What if I'm not good enough? What if they don't like it?" the painter said. "I have to complete the mural, and it has to be perfect. The problem is that I'm struggling to find inspiration. Usually a vibrant image comes into my mind, and I know what I want to paint, but I'm stumped. I'm really at a loss if I'm being up front, and that scares me. If I don't start painting the mural soon, the family will fire me and demand I return the money they paid me. I already spent a lot of it to pay off my debts. There's no way I can return the money they gave me. Everything I have is riding on this mural. I don't know what to do."

The painter ran a hand through his hair, leaned back in his chair, and continued. He felt so comfortable with Valentina. A warm glow emanated off her, and he felt like he was putting his frozen hands up to the heat of a fire. It felt good to talk about his problem, and he was already feeling a small amount of relief from the burden he carried. He was feeling like this sexy librarian could give him the advice he needed and a book to help guide him.

"To be honest, I feel like my creative inspiration left me a year ago. I started feeling depressed more, and life lost its color," the painter said. "Drawing and painting has always been more than a hobby or career. It's been my life's passion. In art, I see the meaning of life, the beauty of creation, and the spirituality of interconnectedness. When I make art, I feel like I'm exploring the cosmos. It's the closest I feel to the divine. When someone buys one of my paintings, I see the happiness and light in their eyes, and it brings me great joy. I love having such a positive influence on people."

"What happened a year ago to make life lose its color, as you said?" Valentina asked. She was sure that a year ago is when Dark Energy infiltrated his life and took hold of his heart.

VALENTINA DZHERSON

"A lot of things happened a year ago. My father died, and while I was grieving, I found out that my wife had been cheating on me with my neighbor. When I confronted her, she left me, which was devastating. I turned to alcohol to numb the pain of everything, and I fell into a deep depression. I still continued to make art because I had to make a living of course, but it wasn't the same. I did not paint from the heart. I no longer painted what I felt. If I had painted what I felt, all my paintings would have been pitch black. I don't drink alcohol any more, but my art hasn't been the same since everything happened. My heart feels heavy, and my mind and soul just can't get back to a place of being inspired by life or love. It's like my heart and soul have ceased to rejoice and any kind of joy feels so far away. Without the power of inspiration, my talent is powerless, and I no longer know where to get my inspiration and where to find my muse," the painter said.

"Once the power of Dark Energy completely overwhelmed him, the inspiration disappeared," Valentina thought to herself. "An intense encounter with Dark Energy will leave a person scarred. Even if they get better as he did, the negativity and oppression of Dark Energy lingers, like a dark cloud following them wherever they go."

"Follow me. I have a book for you," Valentina said, standing up and leaving the reading room. She led the painter to the Spirituality & Religion section of the library and found a good book on spiritual development. When she scanned the book at the checkout counter, she wrote a note on his receipt and stuck it in the front pages of the book, where he would see it. The note had the link to her webcam website and the streaming time for tonight's show. She wrote that it would help him to regain his creative potential through the power of sexuality. The painter thanked her, took his book, and left.

That evening, the painter came home to his empty house, which normally saddened him since it reminded him that his wife had left him. But tonight, he felt hopeful after such a nice and helpful conversation with the sexy librarian earlier in the day. He opened the book and saw the note Valentina had left him. The painter realized that this could be a solution to his inspiration problem, and he immediately logged on to the site, where GG Star's webcam show was already going on.

The painter saw how people gave GG Star an abundance of tips. The tips constantly flowed in because viewers were so pleased with GG Star's presence and performance. It didn't take long for the painter to see why. He was hypnotized by the power of GG Star's sexuality and could not take his eyes off her. At the same time, he felt some kind of new energy awakening in his body. The Dark Energy that plagued his heart started to melt away and left space for Light Energy to return. The painter felt filled with new strength, which was Light Energy, and he looked at GG Star with loving eyes and was overwhelmed with admiration.

GG Star seemed perfect and unique to him, and the painter saw in her something amazing. When he looked at GG Star, he saw his muse, and he immediately wanted to paint his mural. A million different creative ideas came to his mind and flooded his psyche. This surge of creativity had not happened to him for a long time, and it was all thanks to the sexual charge of the superstar webcam performer. She awakened a fountain of creative energy in him through her sexual online performance. The longer he watched, the more the painter felt the Dark Energy inside him recede. He became kinder and his love of life returned. It was like he could see the colors of the world again. His inner balance was restored and Light Energy reclaimed his soul. In gratitude to GG Star, the painter left a good tip on her website and enthusiastically set to work sketching out and planning his mural for the room in the rich family's mansion.

That night, in addition to this painter, other people received similar life-changing healing. There were more than 10,000 other people around the world who, like him, received a powerful charge of GG Star's sexual energy and inspiration. They fell in love again, they felt a surge of strength and positive energy within them, they were cured of the influence of Dark Energy, and they found inner balance and peace. Each of GG Star's viewers fell in love with life again, wanted to live happily, and create something positive with their lives. All of them thanked GG Star from the bottom of their hearts with tips, each at their discretion.

As her webcam performance ended, GG Star signed off and blew her audience a kiss goodnight. Once again, Ivan was awestruck at how much money they made that night. He told Valentina that he would be giving her a raise and that she'd be making an even bigger percentage of their profits. Valentina was happy of course, but that night she was thinking more about her mission. She realized the huge potential that existed in her sexual energy if she invested it in the people who needed it. She was looking forward to seeing the painter again when he eventually came to the library to return the book, and she could hear how he enjoyed her webcam performance and how his mural was going.

When she got back to her apartment that night, Valentina poured herself a glass of red wine and sat on the couch. Patrul jumped up beside her and purred as she pet him. She thought back to how she had helped the painter and how his mural would inspire and heal others. On that day, Valentina's mission was accomplished and she felt excellent. She was also very glad that by doing good to people, she was able to make excellent money for her human life on Earth and live comfortably. Full of joy and happiness, she went to bed. Her human body needed rest and strength for the next day of work in the library and on the webcam website in the evening.

※

Chapter 12

THE PROFESSOR

After a restful weekend of exercising, cooking, and spending time outdoors with Patrul, Valentina went back to work on Monday. Like all other humans, she had to work. However, unlike many humans, Valentina enjoyed her jobs and had a greater purpose than merely earning money to survive. In both her work as a librarian and webcam performer, she was slowly but surely saving the world from Dark Energy and restoring The Great Balance in the universe. After a few months, she had already healed thousands of people and set them up on a journey of Light Energy, peace, and harmony within themselves.

Work at the library was usual for a Monday. There weren't as many people on Mondays as other days of the week, so Valentina enjoyed a quiet start to her day. The workload was slow, so she even sat in a comfy chair and read a book with Patrul curled up on her lap. Sometime in the afternoon, a library customer arrived, and Valentina met him at the checkout desk.

"Here is another soul to save," Valentina thought to herself when she got a look at him. *"I can almost see the Dark Energy swirling around him. It's like a millstone hanging around his neck, threatening to drown him. I must do something to alleviate his pain and suffering."*

The customer was a professor at the local university, and he was also the head of the history department. Valentina recognized him from her brief time as a university student. She thought she remembered seeing his face on a flyer advertising a history lecture. The professor was one of the university's most prominent instructors, and she remembered someone telling her that he was famous in Tomsk for his brilliant mind. He was well-regarded in his field of history. Valentina was glad she had the opportunity to heal someone so influential. If she could help rid his soul of Dark Energy, the professor could be a force for good on campus, showering Light Energy to his students and other faculty members.

"Good afternoon, are you free at the moment, miss?" the professor asked.

He was an old man in his late sixties with a bald head that he covered with an old-fashioned cap. He wore a brown tweed jacket and round glasses. His white mustache fit him well, and he twirled the edges with wax, so Valentina could tell that he cared about his appearance and took pride in how he looked. He did look good for his age, she noticed. However, there was a sadness in his eyes that was evident.

"My job is to help customers like you, so of course I'm free," Valentina said with a smile that made the professor blush. She could tell he was shy around her because she was a gorgeous, sexy librarian much younger in age than him. "Are you looking for any specific book in particular?" she asked.

"I'm looking for a book, any book really, that will please my soul," the professor said. "You see, my work at the university is my life, and I enjoy it a great deal. But when I come home from work, I want something different to occupy my mind. Instead of history and facts and figures, I want something that brings me joy and pleasure. Do you have any books that could do that for me?"

"I'm sure we can find a book that will give you pleasure and the passion that you're craving," Valentina said. "What exactly makes your soul happy, if I may ask?"

At that moment, the old professor blushed again, and Valentina could tell he was on the brink of telling her something very personal and secret about himself. He hesitated though, and she sensed he was unsure if he could trust her with such private information. She knew she had to act fast before she lost her chance to help him.

"Professor, I assure you that as a librarian, I'm very accustomed to hearing sensitive information," she said, leaning over the desk in a way that accentuated her breasts through her fashionable, tight-fitting shirt. "You can trust me. Anything you tell me will stay with me, I promise. You have my word." Valentina smiled gently at him, careful not to overdo her charm.

"Well, all right," the professor said with a twinkle in his eye. His tense shoulders relaxed and he exhaled. It actually would feel very good to get this off his chest and tell someone. "Perhaps we can continue our conversation over tea?" he asked politely.

Valentina agreed and told him to wait for her at a nearby table while she brewed some. Soon, she brought out two hot cups of tea, they sat down, and the professor began to explain his predicament to her.

"What I'm going to tell you can never leave this table because of my position at the university. If word got out about my personal life and inclinations, I fear my job would be in jeopardy. People would misunderstand or misinterpret my desire. They would twist it into something that it's not. The truth is I have a lot of shame about my true desire. I've kept it hidden for a long time, but it feels like it's slowly killing me, like I'm drinking a small amount of poison every day," the professor said, then took a sip of tea before continuing.

"I'm already 68 years old, and I've been married and divorced twice now. I have adult children who are living independently in Moscow. They don't need me anymore of course, but they still include me in their lives, which I'm grateful for. I live alone, and I'm afraid I'm an incredibly lonely man. This is where my secret desire comes in," the professor said. "To be honest, even though I'm an older man, I still love to see young, beautiful women. Like the college-aged students I teach. The university is full of young women who are 19 or 20, and their beauty makes my heart go pitter-patter. Seeing their beauty and being so close to their charming energy brings me great joy. At this point in my life, young, beautiful women are the only thing that makes my soul fly. I know I'm an old man, and some would say it's shameful that I want to flirt with women so much younger than myself, but it's simply the truth. I've kept my desires hidden for so long, and I've become so unhappy with life. I want to give in to my desires and be happy again. Is that so wrong?"

Valentina put her hand on his and caressed it.

"Of course not. It's only natural to be drawn to beauty, no matter the age," she said, reassuring him. She could tell that even just saying the words out loud had done a great deal to lift the weight of Dark Energy off his shoulders. Her work wasn't done yet though. There was much more healing in store for this lonely, old man. "What exactly do you want from these young women?" she asked.

The professor got very red in the face and felt embarrassed. He cleared his throat and answered Valentina.

"Obviously, I would love to touch and kiss them, but I'm not stupid. I understand how old I am and how that's not a viable possibility at my age. I certainly could not give a young woman enough physical pleasure from sex. My body just isn't able to do that anymore," the professor explained. "So I'm not looking for any sex or physical intimacy with young women. Those days are behind me. But I would still like to spend time in their presence and feel their charm and youthfulness. I would be happy chatting with them over tea, like we're doing now. Or chatting with them from afar even. I would like to be able to tell a young woman how beautiful she is and how perfect her body is. Just talking to a young woman about sexuality and sexual things would be more than enough for me. It would make me feel young again. I would be able to feel that excitement and pleasure from them that I long for and have denied myself for so many years."

"And now you've come to the library for a book to help you re-connect with young women somehow and indulge your deepest desire?" Valentina asked. The wheels in her mind were already turning about which book to give the professor and how to help him. She was about to change his life for the better. Today was the first day of a happier, more fulfilled life with more passionate, in-spiring Light Energy and less depressing, confining Dark Energy.

"In a perfect world, I would find a beautiful young woman to talk to and appreciate. I would like to enjoy her presence and company, and just having the chance to spoil her would make me feel amazing. With my prominent position at the university, I make good money, more than I could ever spend on myself. My life is very simple, so I have lots of excess money that I wish I could spend on a beautiful young woman. But I have no idea how I would ever find someone who would agree to my idea or how I would get in touch with someone would want to meet me," the professor said. "Instead, I came here looking for a book that would be the next best thing. Something that would mimic the experi-ence. Perhaps a romance novel. I guess that's where you come in. Do you have any suggestions or book recommendations for me?"

When the professor finished his story, he was so surprised by what he let himself tell this stranger. He fought the urge to feel shame about what he had disclosed to her and how he had opened up about something so personal and private. He knew he could trust this sexy librarian, and he felt hopeful that she could help him with his problem.

"Wait right here. Give me a few minutes to find a book for you," Valentina said.

She left to find something right for him. She came back with an old-fashioned steamy romance novel. The professor looked delighted by it. On the first page, she put a small piece of paper where she had written her website address for him to join to-

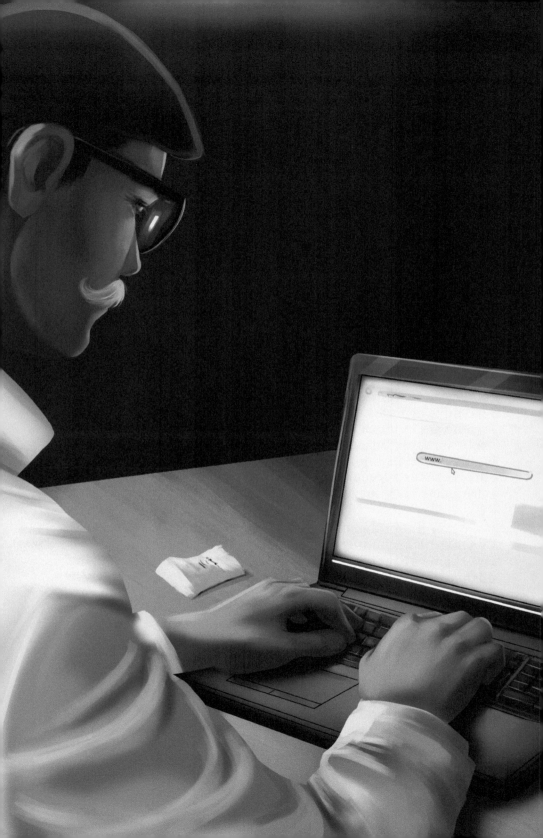

night's webcam show. The professor thanked Valentina and headed to the university where he was supposed to be preparing for a lecture the next day. As he left the library, the professor looked around nervously, hoping that no one had heard his story by chance. He did not understand how Valentina's strong influence made him tell the whole truth of his desire. It was, of course, the influence of sexual power from her superpowers as GG Star that made him feel so comfortable and pulled out his honest, raw self when they talked over tea. The professor did realize how young and attractive Valentina was, and he felt that he wanted to return to the library soon, just to see her again. He relished the opportunity to communicate with such a beauty.

In the evening when he got home, the professor opened the book that he got in the library and found the website that was written on the piece of paper. He decided to check it out, so he logged onto the webcam website. At that moment, GG Star's live show was at its peak. GG Star was absolutely on fire in her performance. She was in the zone, touching her body and giving an incredible and unforgettable performance for the viewers. The professor saw how many people were sending tips for her amazing performance. He had never visited any kind of erotic website before and at first, he did not know what to do. He just sat there, watching GG Star's show with admiration and noticing how other members were acting in the chat online.

The professor could not believe his secret desire had come true that day. He typed her a message in the private chat with compliments on how beautiful and young she looked. GG Star answered back to him immediately with her gratitude for the nice compliment. His heart leapt for joy, and it started beating faster and stronger in excitement. The professor started to fall in love with what he saw, and Light Energy started activating in his body and filling him up. The Dark Energy that previously consumed him started to go away until his spirit regained harmony and balance. He felt an amazing change in his spirit and in his body on a physical level. He felt such happiness and joy, all thanks to the sexual energy of GG Star. He sent her massive tips for this physical, emotional, and spiritual relief.

Even after GG Star's show, the professor still couldn't get her out of his head. He laid in bed, still thinking of her performance. The most attractive thing about her performance was the fact that GG Star acted so natural and free in her sexuality, and he saw real joy on her face in her self-satisfaction. The facial expression at the moment of her orgasm was like a drug, bringing emotional pleasure to all the viewers. This was how he achieved balance inside him, and life was never the same again. He never experienced the unhappiness he had before meeting Valentina as the sexy librarian and GG Star as the webcam performer. The professor regularly tuned into GG Star's webcam performances. He got the sexual healing therapy he needed from her powerful erotic energy, which not only helped him, but also helped thousands of other people around the world.

※

Chapter 13

THE YOGA INSTRUCTOR

Ten years had passed since Valentina started working at the library in Tomsk. In those ten years, she had met so many people and saved so many lives. Valentina felt like it was time to move on to some other place, as it was becoming obvious that she wasn't getting older. Her body wasn't aging at all and people were beginning to ask her about her secret to not aging. Others grew suspicious, and her youthfulness became a topic of conversation among library employees, customers, and the other tenants in her apartment. Valentina never disclosed her true identity of course and kept the people around her in the dark. In order to hide her magical power and her true nature, she needed to find another place to live where no one knew her. It was time to start over.

Another reason to move was so many customers kept going to the library just to see her and get attention. Per usual, people fell in love with Valentina without her even trying, and they became intoxicated by her charm and wouldn't let her go. She got bored of these obsessive people, as she didn't need human attention at all. She only used them for her own sexual pleasure on occasion.

Even when Valentina was having sex with some humans, they got kind of addicted to her and became annoying. When she was created, she was not programmed for love, so she did not enjoy these human attachments.

Valentina packed up her apartment and told Ivan that she was quitting. He was devastated because she alone had tripled his business. She was the main moneymaker for his webcam business, and with the revenue from her performances, he had moved to a much bigger and nicer studio and hired more performers. Even though the other women studied Valentina's shows, they could never fully imitate her sexual power that was gifted to her by Mother Venus and the Gods. Ivan understood that she had to move on from this city, so he wished her well and paid her the final payment from her last performance.

Valentina moved with Patrul from Tomsk to St. Petersburg. Living in a bigger city excited her because she knew that a bigger city came with more opportunities to save people, plus with such a large population, she wouldn't stand out as much as she had in Tomsk. She found another library, where she would work by day, and by night she continued her superhero mission of saving the world. With all her income, she was able to start her own webcam website, and all her viewers from Ivan's website followed her. She was her own boss, and it felt good to be in control of her life and be completely financially independent.

Valentina worked six days a week, and on her day off, she enjoyed keeping to herself, exploring the city, and having fun on her own. She got such joy and excitement from visiting new places. Work went smoothly, and she quickly adjusted to the new library, which was much bigger than her old one. The new library in St. Petersburg was run by a director named Mr. Morozov, who was a tall, slender man who always dressed in a black suit. He was middle-aged and handsome, but his piercing dark eyes made him seem less than inviting. There was definitely an element of mystery and intrigue with him. Valentina could sense something was interesting about Mr. Morozov, but she couldn't identify it.

The director was very kind to her, but never in a warm way. Mr. Morozov's kindness felt icy, even if he was being polite. He tried to talk to her every possible moment, always offering some help if she needed anything. Mr. Morozov tried to advise her on everything, even when she did not ask. He was a polite, but pushy old man. Valentina was used to her supervisor giving her a lot of leeway and freedom to work independently, so she was not accustomed to such close supervision from her boss. She knew she was a capable, competent worker, so she didn't mind the supervision. Valentina did not take Mr. Morozov's pushiness and overbearing personality too seriously, but Patrul was kind of nervous whenever he came around. The black cat did not like Mr. Morozov one bit, but, like Valentina, could not identify why.

One day at the library, a young good-looking woman came in and approached Valentina. The woman was athletic and fit, and she told Valentina that she was a yoga instructor. She asked Valentina where she could find books on tantra.

"I know Tantra is an ancient practice that's about celebrating your body and feeling a heightened sensuality. It intertwines spirituality, sexuality, and a state of mindfulness," Valentina said, recalling information from her free time reading books at her previous library. "If I remember correctly, traditional tantra has two parts: white tantra and red tantra. White tantra is the solo practice, which involves yoga and meditation. The goal of white tantra is to create a deeper bond with yourself. Red tantra is the sexual practice, and the goal is creating a deeper bond with your partner. Is that right?"

"That's right," the yoga instructor said shyly, brushing a strand of hair behind her ear. Valentina could tell the woman felt self-conscious to be talking so openly about sex in public. This was another person who had Dark Energy inhabiting them, and it was negatively affecting her life and holding her back.

"Which tantra are you interested in learning about?" Valentina asked. "White tantra or red tantra? Are you interested in getting to know yourself better or your partner better?"

"I want to try white tantra first, and then maybe move onto red tantra," the yoga instructor said quietly, avoiding eye contact with Valentina. "That is, if I can find the right partner."

It was clear that the woman looked somewhat confused, and her breathing became irregular. It didn't take someone with superpowers like Valentina to tell that something was bothering her. Valentina looked into her eyes and wondered what her secret desire was. The yoga teacher took a deep breath and held it for a few seconds to calm herself down. Then she lifted her face up, looked at Valentina, and told her story.

"I have to admit that I'm a bit confused at the moment. I have been for a few months now. My mind feels all mixed up," the yoga instructor said. "I don't quite understand my own feelings."

"Tell me more. I'm sure a listening ear will do you good, plus I can help you find the perfect book to help you with what you're going through," Valentina said.

"Okay. Well, I have almost entirely female students. When my class is full of female students and I'm leading the lesson, my eyes wander. I involuntarily gaze at the beautiful curves of the women's bodies as they hold themselves in various positions. They are like gorgeous statues before me," the yoga instructor said. "When one of my students struggles with the pose or needs help, I come up to them and correct their pose. Of course, this involves me touching their bodies. My hands might be on their hips, their arms, or their legs. It can be very intimate and sensual in a way. The moment I feel any kind of intimacy, I don't want it to ever end. It feels so good, like a delicious flavor I've never tasted or an exotic flower I've never seen."

The yoga instructor cleared her throat, took a deep breath, and continued.

"Although I've been happily married to my husband for seven years, I can't fight these new feelings anymore. I can't ignore the fact that I have a deep attraction to women. I also feel strange when, after the lessons, my students come up to me to thank me for the excellent class, and they hug me in gratitude for their emotional and physical relaxation. In general, this is a normal process, and it's common in yoga classes because we grow to know each other well. I understand their feelings, but I want to linger in their hugs for a little longer than necessary. I crave the sweet female energy exchange," the yoga instructor said. "Every time I touch a beautiful woman for a moment, I want it to last longer, but the situation doesn't allow me to. I need to adhere to professional ethics. I also don't want the students to suspect that I have any additional feelings for them or get the wrong impression."

"Do you want a romantic or sexual relationship with a woman?" Valentina asked. She needed to go deeper, and get at the heart of the woman's desires in order to heal her and set her free from the Dark Energy of doubt and resistance to her true pleasure.

"No, I don't want any kind of relationship with a woman, but I have this intense desire to touch them and caress their skin. It hasn't gone away. I'm very ashamed to admit this to you, even though you're being so understanding and nonjudgmental. No one else knows this, not even my closest friends or my husband," the yoga instructor confessed. "Such private topics are not accepted in my social circles, and they can even provoke conflict or misunderstanding. Based on principle, I don't fantasize about sex with other women, but I am still interested in other women. However, there's no way to experiment with a woman or satisfy my desire. I'd like to find out what exactly I want from them."

Valentina understood exactly what she meant. The yoga instructor had these desires and wanted to explore them, but she didn't want to do it in a way that broke her vows to her husband or caused a rift between them. She left to retrieve a book about tantra, and she also got a book about female bisexuality too. The book had clear explanations about what bisexuality was, what types of bisexuality exist, and ideas of how to explore one's bisexuality. Both books together would let the yoga instructor learn about herself. Valentina also snuck in a note with her website on it in case the woman was interested in watching her performance.

Valentina and the yoga instructor didn't realize it, but they hadn't been alone this whole time. Their conversation had not

been private like they assumed it was. The director had been secretly listening to them behind the door. Suddenly, Mr. Morozov leaned on the door accidentally and it creaked, alerting them to someone's presence. Valentina and the yoga instructor realized they were not alone, and the woman left fast without even thanking the sexy librarian who had helped her a great deal.

Valentina was beginning to think that something strange was going on with the director, and she got a bad feeling about him. Patrul was glad that she finally shared his wariness about Mr. Morozov. She did not like the energy in the air when he was around. She sensed Dark Energy in him, like most normal people, but the Dark Energy in him was different somehow. She couldn't put her finger on it. Valentina had never met anyone with such mysterious energy before. She wasn't happy that Mr. Morozov had been spying on them, and she told him that it was rude to eavesdrop. Mr. Morozov shrugged it off and claimed that he had been looking for a book in the back, but it was obviously untrue. Valentina had to keep her identity as GG Star a secret from humans, so she made a mental note to be more careful next time and make sure the director wasn't listening to any conversations with customers.

That evening, the yoga teacher felt very curious when she opened the book about bisexuality and saw the address of a website that looked like an adult site. She opened her laptop and checked it out. GG Star was already online, and her chat was open and available for anybody. She started with soft and slow teasing, and erotic dancing while she answered the people's messages in the public chat. The yoga instructor saw that GG Star was very communicative with her audience and answered every single message even if it was only "Hi." With shaking hands, the yoga instructor typed a message saying hello and complimenting her performance so far. GG Star said hi to her by looking into the camera and using the woman's username. The yoga teacher blushed and felt very special, which made her feel more confident and brave too.

She took a deep breath and clicked the button to invite GG Star to a private chat room for a chance to sext privately. GG Star accepted the invitation, and they both disappeared from the public area. GG Star felt like she should lead the conversation, so she took control. She smiled and performed for the yoga instructor, teasing, slowly undressing, and gently touching herself. In the beginning, the woman was very quiet, but the more naked GG Star got, the more compliments the yoga teacher gave her. After several minutes of GG Star openly playing with herself, she climaxed in full view of the camera. At that very moment, the yoga instructor climaxed too without even touching herself. She realized that she really was a bisexual person, and her fears and apprehension fell off her like shackles of Dark Energy.

The yoga instructor really enjoyed sexting with a woman. She appreciated female sexuality, and she felt like she discovered the solution to her dilemma. GG Star's webcam performance was enough for her to feel excited and happy, but most importantly, she could satisfy her emotional needs and sexual curiosity in a very safe way. No one knew she had visited the adult website and was sexting with GG Star. It was a totally private exchange. The experience that night helped her learn about her own sexuality. The yoga instructor finally understood herself and started to feel peace and harmony inside her heart. Not only did the yoga teacher get relief and sexual energy from the performance, but GG Star had awakened her bisexuality. The woman's bisexual energy was blocked before and could not find a way out because of fears stemming from social and moral norms and her own insecurity. But once the yoga instructor saw how GG Star came hard for her, all her shame and fear disappeared!

That day, one more person received emotional and sexual freedom and satisfaction. The yoga instructor began a new and exciting life, full of the most important inner peace and balance. GG Star felt happy to have helped another person, plus she made great money as the private chat was twice the price of the public chat.

✳

Chapter 14

THE SURGEON

A week later, Valentina was in the library again working, as usual. She scanned the returned books, put them back on the correct shelves, and tidied up the library. She tried to avoid the director as much as possible, but he sometimes found her and kept tabs on her. Valentina's favorite part of her job was speaking to customers and helping people get the right book. Even though the working conditions weren't as simple and easy as the library in Tomsk, she was happy to work here at a bigger library in St. Petersburg because more people were exposed to her superpowers. Completing her mission to heal people and rid the earth of the overpowering Dark Energy was important, and putting up with the annoying and overbearing Mr. Morozov was worth it in the long run. Over the years, Valentina had experienced a few more dreams in which Mother Venus told her that she was on the right path and doing a good job, so she came to the library with a positive attitude every day, ready to help whoever walked in.

That day, it was raining, and there weren't many customers in the library. Valentina watched as a tall and serious-looking man walked in and shook off the rain from his umbrella. The man wore blue scrubs, so she could tell that he worked in the medical field. His face was kind of sad, and he was lost in his thoughts, concentrating hard. The man's body was tense, and Valentina could sense how much pressure and stress he held in his shoulders and back. If she was alone with him, she knew that a sensual massage would do wonders for him, but she had to remain professional. Plus, she didn't want him to fall in love with her and become obsessive like other men had in her past. The serious man approached the desk and greeted Valentina.

"I was wondering if your library has any books about rehabilitation after heart surgery," the man asked.

"I take it you work in a hospital?" Valentina asked.

"Yes, I'm a surgeon I'd like to get a book for one of my patients," the surgeon said.

"Wow, being a surgeon is an important job. You hold people's lives in your hands. You change your patients' lives with the work you do for them," Valentina said genuinely. She admired his healing work, as she was also a healer, albeit in a different way. While the surgeon focused on people's physical health, Valentina focused on their emotional, mental, sexual, and spiritual health. Even though their methods weren't the same, she still was happy to meet a fellow healer, despite him not having any superpowers like her.

"Thanks for the kind words," the surgeon said with a weak smile, but then his face turned cloudy. "That's the problem though. My work is so important that it can be extremely stressful and taxing. I'm emotionally and physically drained most of the time,"

"You want a book about rehabilitation after heart surgery, correct? Did you operate on someone recently?" Valentina asked. She was curious to know more about the surgeon's emotional state and what his true desires were, but she sensed that he needed to warm up to her first. Unlike others, the surgeon was more guarded and wouldn't disclose such personal matters without feeling more comfortable with the sexy librarian.

"Yesterday, I completed a successful surgery on a friend of mine. I don't normally treat people I know, but this was an emergency surgery. If we didn't act soon, his heart would've malfunctioned," the surgeon said. "I was the only cardiothoracic surgeon at the hospital, so I rushed into the operating room. My friend is resting now, but I'd like to get him a motivational book. He has a long road to full recovery."

"How did the surgery go?" Valentina asked. She saw how extremely tense the surgeon was, and how abruptly he spoke. He was very frazzled and exhausted. Something about this surgery had tipped him over the edge, and he was spiraling into darkness.

"Well, the surgery was successful. I'm a very talented surgeon and I'm incredibly careful, so I hardly ever have unsuccessful surgeries," the surgeon said. "However, this one was a close call. Since it was my friend, I was more nervous than usual. My hands were shaking. My surgical assistants had never seen me like that before, and it threw them off. One of them handed me the wrong size knife, and I almost used it. If I hadn't caught myself right before I made the incision, it could have been terrible. The knife was too large for his heart, and it would've cut too deep and ruptured his heart. Thankfully, I realized the surgical assistant's mistake and got the correct knife."

"That sounds very stressful," Valentina said.

"It was. I almost collapsed at the end of the surgery because I was so intensely focused and determined not to make any mistakes. It took all my willpower to complete the surgery," the surgeon said. "I've been working a lot at the hospital, saving the lives of people every day by performing surgeries. I've never regretted my career, but I have felt the heavy weight of responsibility. It's crushing at times. I'm not allowed to make even a small mistake because it could cost the lives of my patients. This is why I always feel a huge amount of tension in my head and body. It feels like an elephant is sitting on my chest, and I can hardly breathe at times.

I dream of finding a way to release it. I desperately want to feel peace and harmony inside myself, even if only for a single day. Nothing would make me happier."

The surgeon sighed and slicked back his wet hair before continuing.

"My career is my life, so I don't have any outlet to release my stress and the crippling weight of responsibility. I carry such a fear of failure in me. Since I'm always on call, I simply have no time to spend doing anything for myself. Medicine is my whole life, and I consider it my duty to save people, but sometimes I feel like I also need help. I wish I had someone looking after and taking care of me. I wish I had someone to give me inner peace and some new inspiration. Sure, I feel happy after each surgery with a positive outcome, but soon that happiness disappears, and I feel empty inside. I have no inspiration, and I feel like I've had the life sucked right out of me."

"You've come to the right place," Valentina said, knowing that the surgeon was describing exactly what Dark Energy does to its victims. "Wait here while I look for some books."

Valentina had a good understanding of what he needed. She brought two books: one motivational book about rehabilitation after heart surgery for his friend and one book about meditation for him. She put a note with her website information inside the book for the surgeon, and she handed them both to him.

"I have another suggestion that might help you before your surgeries," Valentina said before the surgeon left.

"What's that? I'm all ears," he said.

Just then, Valentina heard a low vibration at her side. She turned and saw that Patrul was aggravated, and he was emitting a low growl. Something was wrong. She followed Patrul's gaze, and she saw that once again, the director of the library was listening to the conversation. Valentina couldn't believe he was eavesdropping again! She didn't feel like she should scold him again because he was her superior after all. She didn't want him

to know that she noticed his presence. Valentina wanted to have the upper hand in the situation.

"What's your advice?" the surgeon asked, and Valentina turned back to face him. She had been distracted by the realization of Mr. Morozov eavesdropping that she had forgotten that she was about to tell the surgeon an important tip.

"Give me one moment. I'll jot it down for you," Valentina said, not wanting to say it out loud and have Mr. Morozov overhear it. No one could find out about her secret identity, and her sexual wisdom would be a big clue for them to find out. On a piece of paper, she wrote "Try masturbating before surgery. Masturbation relaxes the mind and body, and it will help you focus." She handed the paper to the surgeon.

"Ah yes, that's a good idea," the surgeon said. He wasn't embarrassed at the talk of sexual things since he was accustomed to talking about all sorts of taboo topics in the medical setting. He thanked her and left.

Valentina pretended to tidy up the desk for a few minutes before walking away toward the other end of the library. She knew Mr. Morozov was watching her, and she didn't want him to find out she knew he had been eavesdropping. Patrul followed her, and they spoke to each other telepathically.

"Can you believe he was eavesdropping again? I made sure he wasn't around when the conversation with the surgeon started," Valentina said in her head.

"He appeared halfway through the conversation. The director is very sneaky. I've always known something is strange about him," Patrul told her telepathically. "We need to be extra careful. I will try to investigate and spy on him in the meantime."

"I agree. We need to figure out why he's so nosy, and why his Dark Energy feels different than everyone else's," Valentina thought and focused on finishing the rest of her shift at the library.

When the surgeon got home, he tried to meditate with the book he got at the library. Then, he saw the note Valentina left for him with her website information. He had never used any erotic website like this before, and it made him curious. He logged onto the webcam show, and GG Star was already online performing her erotic show. That night, it was hot as hell and GG Star was on fire. Her magical and powerful sexual energy was like an explosion, and it spread to all the viewers who watched her. She was excited to show off a new sexy outfit one of her viewers had purchased for her, so she was having an especially fun and sensual time.

When the surgeon saw GG Star in the middle of her performance, he was amazed by her beauty and the magic power of her sexuality. Her sexual power touched him immediately and made his heart beat faster. His body was full of excitement, which he had not felt in ages, and now he felt young again and full of motivation. His life energy came back to him in an instant. Like an electric lightning bolt, her sexuality charged him up! He was healed immediately, and the balance of his body and mindset was fixed. The surgeon felt a hundred times better, and he gave GG Star the maximum amount he could tip--all that was in his account.

During the erotic webcam performance, GG Star hit people with her strong sexual power, which came through the camera and directly into people's souls. She brought inner balance and sexual appetite to her viewers from all over the world. Her audience had doubled since she moved to St. Petersburg and launched her own personal website. As it was a public chat performance, thousands of people were healed at the same time. Everyone rewarded GG Star with excellent tips for their healing. The more GG Star healed people, the more power she got in return, and her resources never depleted. Since her fight with the thugs when her energy was depleted, Patrul had trained her to gain positive energy from others. It was a mutual exchange. She could also feed off the positive healing and Light Energy that came off her viewers.

Fighting Dark Energy with her sexual energy, in order to restore inner peace and harmony, was GG Star's mission, and she was doing a damn good job at it. She was very satisfied, sexually and emotionally, after this performance ended. She went to bed feeling like she had done well at her mission and that the thousands of viewers who had watched her sexy performance would never be the same again. They were all healed and also went to bed satisfied with Light Energy in their hearts and souls.

※

PART 4

Evil Beneath the Library

※

Chapter 15

A SINISTER OFFER

In the morning, Valentina went to work like a normal human. Soon, she was again at the library helping people with their problems and helping them find the right books they needed. It was a typical day until something unusual happened that made her understand just how dark and twisted the library director was after all.

As she was helping a customer check out a library book, she suddenly felt a wave of discomfort and unease. Patrul gave her a telepathic signal about Dark Energy approaching from behind her.

"It's coming close, so be on your guard," Patrul told her telepathically. "I'm here if you need me. Steady yourself."

Valentina nodded silently and closed her eyes in concentration. She mentally activated her super protection power, and an invisible barrier of Light Energy formed around her, protecting her from human evil and Black Magic. Even without turning around, she knew where the Dark Energy was emanating from. It was Mr. Morozov. She could recognize his unusual and distinctly creepy Dark Energy anywhere.

"Hello, Valentina," the director said ominously, and she turned to greet him. Normally he appeared charming and pleasant, but today there was no disguising his sinister energy.

Mr. Morozov came closer wearing a fake smile on his face. His mouth stretched as far as it could go, but despite his smile, his eyes were terribly evil.

"Hi Mr. Morozov. What can I do for you?" Valentina asked, keeping calm.

"We need to talk. Come up to my office upstairs as soon as you're free," Mr. Morozov said, then turned and walked upstairs to his office. Normally, his office was strictly forbidden and off limits. Valentina didn't need to be told twice, and she always made sure to stay far away. She wondered what was different about today that she would be allowed inside.

Valentina finished with the last customer and went upstairs where the director was waiting for her. As she climbed the stairs, she spoke to Patrul and told him to wait at the office door just in case she needed him. Valentina knocked on the door and went inside.

Mr. Morozov's office was very dark and suspicious, much like himself. The office had low lighting, and the director's face was partially obscured by shadows. He sat behind his desk in a large leather chair and his piercing eyes glared at her. It was unpleasant for her to be there, and she wanted to start the conversation as soon as possible, so she could quickly leave this place.

Mr. Morozov told her to have a seat, and Valentina sat at a chair across from him. He began the conversation with compliments about her appearance and how beautiful she was. She nodded and thanked him politely, and waited to see where the conversation would go.

"But the most amazing thing about you, Valentina, is not how beautiful you are," Mr. Morozov said. "Do you know what's most amazing about you?"

"I'm not sure, sir," Valentina said. Of course, she knew that her superpowers and superhero status made her amazing. She had been created by the Gods, Devils, Planets, Moon, and Sun after all! Mother Venus's essence was at the very core of her superhero soul. Valentina had never revealed her true superhero nature to any human, and she certainly wasn't going to start now.

"The most amazing thing about you is how easily people trust you with their most secret desires. While they are afraid to tell even the closest people in their lives, people tell you about their secret desires in such detail!" Mr. Morozov said. "Most of these people are ready to take their secrets with them to the grave, but with shocking ease, they tell you the most candid details of their lives. It's incredible, don't you think?"

The director offered her a drink before pouring himself some expensive alcohol. Valentina politely refused because she did not accept alcohol or other kinds of addictive substances. Mr. Morozov took a sip of his drink as he stared at her.

"It's very strange that you don't drink alcohol," he said.

"Why is that?" Valentina said.

"Since you yourself are so addicting. The library customers are addicted to you." Mr. Morozov said with a slimy smirk. "You think I haven't noticed how people are coming to the library more and more often? They come back often for books because of you, if only to see you again. I have been watching you for a long time, and I've noticed that you keep all visitors at a distance. You don't get close, even though people magnetically gravitate toward you. It's a very unusual and powerful skill. I must admit, I'm a bit jealous."

"Is this what you wanted to talk to me about? Do you want me to stop talking to customers about personal matters?" Valentina asked.

"Not at all. Your relationships with customers are great for business. However, I have an idea how your skills can be put for even better use," Mr. Morozov said. He leaned forward, clearly excited about what he was about to propose. The evil in his eyes gleamed brightly in the darkly lit room. "I want to offer you an additional task for your job. Such a young and cute girl like you should not work in the library for the pennies that I pay you. I see in you a strong personality with huge potential to influence people. You can manipulate and control people and their feelings effortlessly. You point direct them in a direction beneficial to you and me. You see, together we could enslave people, force them to do whatever we want, and receive huge sums of money from them. They can become our slaves, and we could dominate them together."

Valentina was very confused and did not like the words he was using and how his energy vibrated. It was clear there was an enormous amount of evil inside him. The director was full of Dark Energy, and it swirled inside him in an aggressive way she had never witnessed in a human before. Mr. Morozov was the kind of person who tried to negatively influence the world to make it even worse.

"Patrul and I were right," Valentina thought to herself. *"Mr. Morozov is a terrible person. Now I see that he's not just creepy. He's incredibly dangerous and hellbent on spreading Dark Energy throughout the world and lording power over people. I can't reject his offer outright just yet. I need to learn more information about his scheme."*

"I can tell you're giving my offer a lot of thought. Surely, it's a lot to take in," the director said with an evil smile. "Instead of just talking about my plan, how about I show you? You can see exactly what kind of business I'm offering to people, and how you could play a role in recruiting more customers. Follow me."

Valentina walked behind Mr. Morozov as they left his office together. They went to the elevator and she watched as he pressed the B button for the basement. She had no idea the library even had a basement. The elevator went down, and they rode in silence. Ever since Mr. Morozov had revealed his sinister offer to her, Valentina could feel his Dark Energy more clearly. There was

so much of it consuming him. He had worked hard to conceal it before, but now that all his cards were on the table, he let it emanate off him without regard. It almost choked her in the small space of the elevator.

The elevator door finally opened, and Mr. Morozov showed Valentina a door at the end of a dim hallway. She felt very uncomfortable, but she did not want to go back. She had to see this through. Being a superhero, she had to confront evil and Dark Energy if she was to save the world from it. They both walked into the room, and the door closed.

It was very dark in the beginning, but still, Valentina followed him. There was one more door, and after she saw many people in a large room. They were coming in from a different entrance of the library, from a secret one. She saw a security guard at the gate collecting money as an entrance fee. Another person gave customers a small package after they paid.

"What's the package they receive when they enter?" Valentina asked.

"It's heavy drugs. Welcome to my sect," the director said, opening his arms and proudly showing off the dingy basement lounge.

Mr. Morozov explained that all his customers were very lonely inside, and for a long time, they had lost all hope. They could not get any inspiration for life or find themselves. They could not hear the inner voice inside themselves that could direct them to a better life. All these people were deeply lost and they didn't have any power inside them to drive their own life and take responsibility. They were like a flock of sheep that accepted and followed any leader. What kind of direction their shepherd was going was not important to them, as they agreed on anything just to get some illusion of happiness.

"All these people are of different ages and social positions, but they all have some money, which they gladly give to me in exchange for some drugs and a sex party," Mr. Morozov told Valentina. "None of them are strong enough to be alone. They're too lazy to find friends or any other kind of long-term relationship. They are always insecure. Just look at them."

Valentina glanced around the large room at all the people sitting at the bar or slouching in booths. They were drinking, smoking, and using drugs. These people were just as the director described them: lost, aimless, hopeless. She could sense their despair and the Dark Energy that drained them of all happiness or agency over their lives. Some of them engaged in sex, but it was not meaningful or tasteful. It was desperate, bad sex that lacked any passion or authentic pleasure. The sect was truly a terrible place.

"Theoretically, they all have a chance to be happy for real, but they are all deeply imbalanced and have no motivation in them to change anything," Mr. Morozov said. "That is why my secret sect business is very successful. The door of my sect is always open for anyone, and they know they can always come back here. Even if they decide to stop one day, as soon as they feel down again, they come crawling back. For me, it is not important who they are. It's only important that they have money and are ready to bring it here. The unhappier people are, the more drugs they are going to buy from me. So for me it is only good if they are always unhappy and deeply out of harmony and balance."

The library director continued, as they walked through the basement between tables and booths.

"As you can see, I can provide them with the space. They can be together here: a great illusion of friendship and unity. They don't feel addicted to the drugs they take here. They call it fun," Mr. Morozov said with a heartless laugh. "So naive. By morning, they crave more. I also allow them to have sex parties with unlimited alcohol. A mix of drugs and alcohol make them feel super down and extremely bad, but they love it because it numbs the emotional pain deep inside themselves. With that much alcohol and drugs in their system, they don't hear their soul crying. On top of that, they happily participate in the dirty sex parties just to feel a small illusion of physical connection with other humans because each of them is so tired of being alone. They like to pretend they love it all. They just want to touch and be touched. But in truth, they don't even enjoy the sex they have here. They are all pretending, and actually many of them don't even feel any physical pleasure since they are under the influence of drugs and alcohol."

"I see," Valentina said quietly as she gazed at a couple having passionless sex in the corner of the room.

"Sure, in the morning, they are going to feel some pain in their genital area from the roughness. They feel healed for a few days and work hard to collect some money for a new party, just to get hurt again and intensify their own personal imbalance. Of course, I'm here for them and always welcome them back. I love money and keeping these people as slaves. They bring all of their savings to me, making me richer. As you can see, they love me a lot. They idolize me. They're afraid to break any of my rules here or offend me because I'm a God to them. Next to me, you could be a Goddess. I really need somebody next to me with a strong and powerful personality, magical beauty, and enough talent to make people believe whatever you say or promise. But the most impressive thing is your powerful sexual energy that works like a magnet and attracts anyone anywhere. Don't you see how you could double my business here?"

Valentina nodded, unsure of how to respond. She didn't want to agree too wholeheartedly because then Mr. Morozov would think she agreed with his sick business. But she couldn't outright disagree with him, or else he might get angry. She needed time to figure out a plan of what to do next with all this new information and the groundbreaking revelation that her boss wasn't who she thought he was.

"I see how perfectly you influence people while you work in the library, but I'm sure your talent deserves a much bigger prize. I know I made the right choice on you, as you never accept any drugs or alcohol, and you're not interested in any swinger party. You're reliable. That's why you would never be influenced by this stuff, so I don't have to worry about you becoming addicted like these people. You're no sad sheep looking for a leader or purpose. I can count on you to steer lost souls here, so we can profit off of their despair. People really love my sect because they see it as a warm home where no one judges them or competes with them.

There is only acceptance and understanding, as they are all the same here. I'm like a strict father with great authority, so they wouldn't dare find any other place like this or take their business elsewhere. My business is always going to be great. Wouldn't it be an honor to be in charge of it with me? To be my helper and a mother to these lost people? Together we could build up a huge empire of sects throughout the world. We could enslave people's minds and free will and become filthy rich in the process."

They got back on the elevator and rode back upstairs. Valentina told Mr. Morozov that she needed a few days to consider his offer. She was shocked to see how deep Dark Energy had infiltrated the director's mind, heart, and soul. She couldn't believe the enormous evil influence he wielded and the speed at which his evil was spreading to large masses of vulnerable people. Mr. Morozov didn't want to save the world and bring balance to the planet, like she did. He wanted to do the opposite. He wanted to make it even worse, and so far he was doing very well! Luckily, he did not know that Valentina was GG Star or about her mission to restore the Great Balance in the world. However, he had obviously detected her powerful energy and sexuality, and he seriously wanted to recruit her into his dark business.

Valentina had to find a way to stop him and bring peace and inner balance to all these lost people from the sect. She had to liberate them from the director's evil grip, so they could be free again.

⁂

Chapter 16

BDSM MISTRESS

The next morning when Valentina arrived at the library, there was already a customer waiting for her at the counter. It was a businessman who came to pick up some kind of motivational book that would take his mind off of business. He worked hard and was very successful at his job, but it sometimes became all-consuming for him and he found himself thinking about business deals and problems in the shower, in bed, or in his free time. He badly needed to relax his mind somehow.

Valentina looked into his eyes and wondered what his secret desire was. He was fascinated by her sexual magnetism and confidence. After a few minutes of talking and gaining his trust like she did with all other customers, the businessman felt at ease. He opened up and told her about his secret desire and how he wanted to fulfill it, even though it made him feel guilty.

"Everything is going well in my life," the businessman said. "I have a top-tier position at my corporation. I am a wealthy, married man, and I have two children. I really appreciate and respect my wife, and she loves me very much. We have a strong marriage. At work, my colleagues and employees respect me. I am a strict, but fair boss. I am the owner of a large construction company. I have a lot of subordinates and clients, and every day I need to solve various issues. Oftentimes, these issues are difficult and complex to solve. It takes a great deal of creativity and intelligence. I control everything myself and am responsible for everything, which can feel like a heavy burden sometimes. However, I'm a good businessman, so my company is developing well and always growing and expanding."

"It sounds like even though your job can be difficult and demanding at times, things are going well in both your business and personal life," Valentina said. "But there's more to it than that, I can tell. Talk to me about your secret desire."

The businessman nodded and leaned in closer, so no other customers could hear their conversation.

"I married for love, and my wife adores me. She is a wonderful mother and mistress of the house, but here's where things get complicated for me," he said, taking a pause before continuing. "I very often have a wild desire to be humiliated and dominated by some very beautiful, fragile, sweet girl. I want her to punish me, and I want to feel beaten. I want her to spit in my face and spank something over my genitals. I want to feel like a small and defenseless person. I just can't do it with my wife. It's not her personality to be so dominant. Even if she could do it, I don't want her to because it wouldn't be as exciting or thrilling. We have a gentle relationship. I really need it to be another girl with strong sexual energy and power. Of course, I would gladly pay for it, but I cannot do it because I promised never to cheat on my wife, and that would be treason. We swore loyalty to each other and I never break a promise. I do not understand where I get this desire, but it sits like a demon inside me and desperately wants to break out! I restrain myself with all my might, but I am tormented by these urges. This strong desire to be punished sexually goes against my promise to be faithful to my wife, and that conflict tears me apart from the inside. I feel such inner turmoil because of this, and it prevents me from living fully."

"I understand completely," Valentina said, nodding. "So much of your life as a businessman involves being in control of everything. You're the decision maker and the boss of everyone. That can take a toll on you emotionally. It sounds like your desire to be humiliated and powerless would be an exhilarating and liberating experience. You could release your burdens and take orders for once."

"Yes, that's exactly how I feel. I can't believe you understand me so well," the businessman said.

Valentina left to find the right book for him to read and learn about this desire. After a few minutes of searching, she came back with a psychology book on sexual fetishes. At the end of the book, she put the name of her website with a personal invitation for him to join. The businessman took the book and was kind of surprised by the name of it. He felt embarrassed about the realization that he had a sexual fetish. He was not sure if it was healthy, but Valentina assured him that it was perfectly normal and natural for people to have sexual fetishes and that everyone's was unique. He left to go back to his job, and Valentina continued working in the library.

All day the director was secretly watching how she did her job and how she communicated with the visitors. Valentina could feel his dark presence behind her back, but she never let him know. She knew she had a few days to figure out how to respond to his sinister offer about joining his sect business, but she was still mulling it over. She avoided him until she could come up with a plan of action.

By the evening, Valentina already knew what the theme of her show would be that night. GG Star would put on a webcam show for BDSM enthusiasts. She knew it was a very popular fetish for many guys, who love to feel the power of a female. It turned them on to feel like they were under the high heels of a strong and dangerous woman. Valentina decided to give them a treat in the public chat, as this fetish was very common. She knew it would be a successful show.

Arriving home, GG Star began her transformation into the BDSM Mistress. She put on black latex lingerie, black stockings, long silk gloves, and patent black high-heeled shoes with red soles. Next, she prepared various punishments for her audience. She pushed the button to go online, and of course, thousands of people from all over the world were already eagerly waiting for her in the chat. Seeing her new sexy, strong image, many of them gasped and their heart rate increased. They could not believe that GG Star knew about their secret desire to be punished! In everyday life, people carefully hid this desire from their spouses, loved ones, and friends. This fantasy was kept locked away in their souls in the hope that no one would know about it or condemn them. But suddenly today fetishists saw that they had a lady who wanted to punish them with pleasure and fulfill their innermost erotic desires!

The bodies of all the site's guests were overwhelmed with lust and admiration. They all waited impatiently for GG Star to assume command over them and order them to do degrading things. They were ready to do anything in order to obey her sexual whims. Regardless, they would be punished, even if they were doing everything well.

Taking the pose of the BDSM Mistress, GG Star ordered everyone to kneel. All the webcam members knelt in front of their computer monitors. As she put her foot very close to the camera and ordered them to lick her heels, thousands of lips reached out to the monitor imitating the worship of her shoes. In everyone's mind there was a fantasy that they were doing it for real in their bedroom and they imagined GG Star in their beds. Next, she ordered them all to take off their pants and get down on all fours like a dog. They all obeyed her order with pleasure, and she began waving and cracking a whip. She hurled words of shame and insult at them, humiliating their dignity. At that moment, the audience members were ecstatic and hoped that GG Star would continue this BDSM performance for a long time.

At this point in the webcam show, the businessman who entered the library in the morning also joined GG Star's chat. He was delighted with what he saw. Without typing anything into the general chat, he just sent her some tips. Next, the businessman quickly took off his pants and obediently began to follow her orders. GG Star continued to humiliate their genitals, wave a whip, and spit at the camera, creating the illusion that it was flying in their faces. They all put their faces closer to their screens because all the audience members were visualizing in their heads that it was happening in reality. Using their imagination, they really experienced authentic emotions of their secret desires being fulfilled. They all felt like they were letting their inner monster out! They idolized GG Star by sending her huge tips to please her and show their gratitude for making their dreams come true.

GG Star continued to give orders, such as making them bark like dogs and engage in physical self-punishment. Most importantly, she made them feel completely subordinate to her, as if they did not have their own free will. She gave them the opportunity to experience all those feelings and emotions that they desperately needed for a long time. These were the feelings that people hid inside themselves because they were afraid. They suppressed these desires until today's amazing performance. GG Star began to slowly undress and tease the webcam members while not allowing them to touch themselves. They could only watch. It was difficult because they desperately wanted to pleasure themselves, but they obeyed. GG Star was so full of sexual charge, and it was torture for them not to touch themselves while watching her show!

GG Star knew exactly what they needed to let off steam and come. She decided to bring their desire to exhaustion through submission and seduction. They were very glad that she understood them and followed her leadership. She intensified their feelings to the maximum, and she satisfied their needs with sexual humiliation. GG Star allowed them to experience this submissive role that they would not have been able to experience in real life. Their inner monsters retreated, and the audience members felt satisfaction and relaxation throughout their bodies, while simultaneously feeling full and at peace. They fed their inner demon by playing a game with GG Star. They were now free and no longer feared any more condemnation or ridicule from the outside since everyone saw how many other people took part in this chat. Everyone realized that they were not alone in their desires and BDSM fetish, and people accepted themselves.

That evening, GG Star made a lot of money as her fans considered it an honor to reward her with the maximum tips. In this way, there were more internally balanced and satisfied people in the world. Thousands of chat members around the world had been rescued from the Dark Energy caused by The Great Imbalance by the strong sexual power and influence of GG Star. Thousands of people that day were cured with a strong sexual charge from the world's superhero. She breathed life into them with her sexual energy, and they were filled with strength. Because sexual energy was the energy of life that gives an impulse to action, the audience was motivated to work. GG Star's burst of sexual energy gave them the strength to bring things to an end, even if things did not work right away. It was sexual energy that gave people perseverance to achieve the final positive result.

Before GG Star's webcam show that night, people were overwhelmed with Dark Energy that suppressed their self-confidence and made them insecure. They were afraid of their own sexual desires and were intimidated by them. Having absorbed the sexual energy of GG Star, thousands of people were filled with sexual power that endowed them with self-confidence, which gave them emotional freedom and acceptance of themselves. As a result, inner harmony came into their souls. GG Star, by giving her sexual energy to people, made progress on her mission to fight against Dark Energy, while making great money for her comfortable human life.

※

Chapter 17

A MESSAGE FROM MOTHER VENUS

After the great webcam show, Valentina took care of her cat Patrul, who was always protecting her from Black Magic or any bad energy from potential enemies. She took a walk around the block to get some fresh air before sleeping, as her human body needed it. She felt proud of the good work she had done helping the businessman and the thousands of others with her performance as a BDSM mistress. She would have to add the BDSM mistress to her repertoire since it was such a huge hit with the audience.

In the morning, Valentina went back to the library to continue her human work helping people find the right books to make their lives happier. Like yesterday, Mr. Morozov again circled around the counter where she worked in order to spy on her and see how she was so good at getting in touch with people's innermost secrets and desires. He could not understand how it was possible for her to so easily get people to tell her such private information. They did so openly, without any shame or worry. The director guessed that Valentina was involved in some form of Black Magic or even hypnosis. Whatever Valentina's secret ability was, he knew it would be great for his evil business of influencing people at the sect.

"I hope you're thinking hard about my offer, Valentina," the director said, emerging from the shadows behind her. Valentina had sensed his presence, but pretended not to because she didn't want him finding out about her superhero abilities. "Have you made up your mind yet? We could amass so much wealth and power together."

"I'm still thinking about it, Mr. Morozov. It's a lot to consider," she said. In truth, Valentina just wanted additional time to learn more about him and how his sect worked. Then, she could find a good way to destroy the evil place and free all the people from his evil grip. She needed a strategy to instill harmony and inner peace inside those poor, lost people by using her sexual super-power.

Before they could continue their conversation, a new customer showed up in the library and Valentina excused herself so she could go help him. The customer was a very old man with a hunched back and cane. She asked him what kind of book he was looking for. The old man said he wanted a travel book with information about faraway destinations and advice for travelers. As she listened to him, Valentina wondered what his secret desire was.

"What's at the root of his interest in travel and escapism?" she thought to herself. After a few minutes of probing further, the old man told her more about himself. They sat down at a nearby table as he explained his story.

"I've never had any problem with money, and I've been lucky to have a good quality of life. I have done a lot of traveling, having adventures, and meeting women," the old man said. "Throughout my life, I have tried many kinds of jobs because I always felt the need to experiment and try something new, or find a new passion. However, since I moved around so much and was never tethered down, I don't have many attachments to anyone. I'm not a very social person when it comes down to it. I don't keep in touch with my friends very well. I also never got married because I never believed in the idea of monogamy, which is why I'm still single at seventy years old."

Valentina could tell that this was where his story would turn more personal, revealing his secret desire. She leaned in as he continued.

"I have started to feel lonely, and even so I have trouble pushing myself to be more social. I miss private conversations and being helpful and needed by others," the old man said. "I also miss the feeling of excitement and inspiration, like when you have a new goal in life. Of course, I really appreciate the beauty of young women, but it is insane for me to even try to touch them or be intimate with them since I'm too old for that. But, I would be very happy to spoil a young woman with some cash."

When he finished his story, Valentina told him to wait as she left to find a travel experience book with recommendations of which country to visit and in which season of the year, plus how to have fun alone. As usual, she also wrote the address of her webcam website, where she was going to do an inspiring live show and be available for private chatting. The old man thanked her, stood up with the help of his cane, and left the library.

"I couldn't help but overhear your conversation," Mr. Morozov said, approaching Valentina as she sat at the table. " I feel like that old man is perfect for my sect. He is lonely and desiring social connections. At my sect, he could find alcohol, drugs, sex, and companions. He is so vulnerable to becoming addicted to the companionship that he'll spend all his money there. He's such an easy target. I'm sure you can manipulate him into coming downstairs without any issues. You should get him to come to the event we're having tomorrow. It will be our biggest sect party yet. Everyone in the sect will be there. You'll earn a big commission for directly bringing a new member into the sect. You can even visit yourself, like a special guest. I want to introduce you to the members as a powerful woman who should be worshiped there, so you can see how things work. They'll love you, plus you can have some fun too in case you're curious," the director said with a seedy wink.

Valentina had never been so sure that the director was pure evil. She was repulsed by his devious mind and disgusting way of preying on vulnerable people. He lived and breathed Dark Energy, and she could tell by the twinkle in his eye when he winked at her that he had a secret desire to have sex and dominate her, too. Valentina needed to act quickly to make sure his sect ceased its operation and that he was not able to create a new one. She decided it would be smart to visit the sect by herself like a normal guest to spy and gather intel.

"If I wanted to visit the sect tonight, how should I go about visiting? Do I enter through the secret door like everyone else? I think spending time there will help me make my decision," Valentina said.

Mr. Morozov said it was okay as long as she wore a sexy outfit and a vintage mask on her face to preserve her identity. She could also bring her own sex toy for self-satisfaction, in case she was shy and didn't plan on having fun with anyone. He then excused himself to plan the sect's next event, and Valentina continued helping visitors with books.

By the evening, Valentina left for home to get ready for a new hot, sexy webcam show with oil. For this performance, GG Star did not wear any clothes at all and went online totally naked. She slowly and sensually put baby oil all over her sexy body. Again, there was a huge crowd in her chat, and everyone spoiled her with tips for the great performance.

The old man who had visited the library that morning saw her website address and logged onto the webcam performance. He was amazed by GG Star's angelic looks and how pure and natural her behavior was. Being an old man, he was not sure how the chat worked, so he took time to just admire her beauty and sexual performance. To him, the best part was that GG Star actively communicated with her audience and answered the fans easily by text and by voice, looking directly into the camera. The old man

put more money on his account and invited GG Star to the private chat to get to know her better. She accepted the request and left the public chat.

The old man started to give her beautiful compliments about her physical beauty and charm, especially about her powerful, sexy energy that he could feel even through the camera. GG Star was about to play with herself, but he asked her to just sit with him since he just wanted to talk to her. They discussed many things during one hour. He told her his life story and many things about himself. He was wondering about her favorite foods and what kind of animals she preferred because he felt so curious about her.

During this hour the old man felt like new again, like he was ten to twenty years younger. He felt addicted to GG Star's personality. Also, he felt like he had a new friend who was available to talk any time he wanted. It was more than enough for him to feel relieved and young again. He was in love with the cam girl who brought him back to life, and he got so much inspiration from her, like no one had ever inspired him before. With this kind of satisfaction and the illusion of love, the old man felt real peace and harmony inside himself. Every evening, he looked forward to her live show, and his own life got more colorful. GG Star received a lot of money from this private chat and then went back to the public one, where many people were still waiting for her to return.

After her show, Valentina thought a lot about the sect, and she asked Mother Venus for help. Hopefully, she could give her some advice or maybe some extra power that she could use against the director. She had only used her superpowers on such a large group of people over the webcam. To defeat the sect, she would need to use her superpowers on a large group of people in-person, and she was unsure of how to do so, which is why she needed Mother Venus' help. When Valentina was asleep in bed, she had a beautiful dream full of tenderness, passion, love, and desire. She felt the entire spectrum of good emotions, and Mother Venus came to her with a warm hug. Mother Venus came to give Valentina more inspiration and belief in herself, along with more confidence in her superpower.

"GG Star, you are full of power by day and by night," Mother Venus said. "You can influence humans in front of the camera and in-person. Your powers stay strong in front of people. Also, you can heal even just a single person who is front of you in real life, but for this you need to learn how to control your own superpower to avoid accidently burning someone or making them sick or addicted to your sexual energy. Remember, GG Star, your mission is healing humans by your sexual superpower, not making slaves of them for your own sexual desire. Understand that you're a superhero day and night. It is your soul that's connected with your human body, and it is not separate."

"How can I control my sexual power? How do I activate it fully?" Valentina asked.

"Always be authentic and unique in your emotions and feelings. Always let negativity go and never pretend," Mother Venus said. "Sexuality and erotism is your nature, so never hide or push it down. The GG Star that makes up your soul possesses an enormous, endless, unlimited power of sexual energy. This energy was given to you to defeat evil. You should not worry, since you are strong enough to defeat your enemies. You must fully feel your power, learn how to manage it, and correctly direct it to people, so your healing power can penetrate deep into their souls, minds, and hearts. To be able to heal people, it is necessary to beam your energy of sexuality into people so they feel its warmth and gain strength. Then, with enough Light Energy inside them, they can resist Dark Energy if it starts to penetrate them again."

"I understand," Valentina said as she listened to Mother Venus' advice.

"It's more powerful if you naturally let out your erotism and sexual healing energy instead of forcing it. You need to practice how to manage your superpowers because you will need to be as effective as possible when you visit this sect. Open yourself up in front of the crowd and heal all these humans energetically. The activation of sexual energy begins in a very natural way through sexual attraction and feelings of self-eroticism," Mother Venus explained. "Sexual arousal begins in your body, emanating from your genes and spreading throughout the body, until it overwhelms you with a powerful charge of sexuality. That charge finds a way out through the skin and glows with a bright, lilac light around your body like a magical aura that hits people and heals them. The bright, lilac light fills the void in their souls and gives them inner strength and harmony!"

Valentina was beginning to feel more confident about her plan to infiltrate and destroy the sect's power over the lost and lonely people.

"When you are in the center of the sect, if you suddenly have doubts or if fear grips you, imagine that you have already defeated evil. Just remain yourself and act as confidently as possible, since your sexual superpower is much stronger than Dark Energy," Mother Venus said. "But be careful. Show your magical power only when it is necessary to fight evil and heal people. So much evil has appeared on planet Earth, and evil forces want to completely destroy humanity by zombifying it, pumping it with Dark Energy, enslaving people, forcing them to submit to evil forever! GG Star, listen closely. One of the representatives of evil is the director of the library where you work during the day. You must hurry in defeating him, as there are more and more such villains, and you must defeat them all. Otherwise, they will be able to unite and create a more powerful evil that would be difficult to defeat, even for a superhero like you, GG Star. Godspeed and good luck!"

Mother Venus hugged Valentina and left as the dream faded, leaving Valentina with clear instructions for her mission.

※

Chapter 18

THE SECRET PLAN

Valentina woke up feeling refreshed and focused the next morning. She remembered her dream and all the advice and encouragement Mother Venus had given her in preparation for her takedown of the evil director's sect. As long as she played it cool and didn't let anyone know about her secret plan, Mr. Morozov wouldn't see her superpowers coming. He wouldn't expect a superhero like GG Star to infiltrate his underground sect and put an end to twisted manipulation of lost people in the name of Dark Energy. He told her that tonight was a huge event at the sect, and that everyone in the sect would be there to party. It was the perfect opportunity for her to liberate as many people as possible from the sect and the clutches of Dark Energy. Today was a big day in her life as a superhero, so Valentina made sure to eat a good breakfast. She would need all the energy she could get to pull off her secret plan.

Making extra breakfast had put her behind schedule, so Valentina rushed out the apartment door and quickly made her way to the library. As she was hurrying, she briefed Patrul on her talk with Mother Venus and the plan for tonight. She told Patrul that she would need extra protection from Dark Energy and Black Magic, so he should be on high alert and monitor Mr. Morozov's every move until she could clock out and return home to prepare for her infiltration of the sect.

It was a new day at the library, and Valentina had to try to save as many human souls as possible. Normally, she was calm and talking to customers came easily to her, but today her body buzzed with anticipation for tonight's mission. Valentina took deep breaths and centered herself, so she could focus on getting through her shift. Even though she was waiting to infiltrate the sect tonight, she still had an opportunity to help customers today.

The first customer that sought out her help was a computer geek. He was a cute guy who was slightly overweight and had curly hair. He said he was a university student and in order to get ready for an exam, he needed the books on his list. The computer geek didn't look very happy and did not have much life energy inside him. Valentina was surprised by his low levels of life energy because usually young people his age have an abundance of it. She knew that something must be going on with him for his life energy to be so depleted. Valentina took the book list, looked at him in the eyes, and wondered what his secret desire was. She was sure that his secret desire was at the root of his problems and low life energy. Since he couldn't fulfill his secret desire or was confused by it, he was depressed and apathetic towards life.

"I can tell something is bothering you," Valentina said to him gently, "and it's not just stress about your upcoming exam. There's something deeper that's troubling you. What is it?"

The computer geek blushed and avoided eye contact with the sexy librarian. It was obvious that she struck a chord and was correct in her assumption.

"I'm fine, really. Even if there was something going on, I would be too shy to talk to you about it anyway," he said. "It's fine. I just need those books on the list, please."

"It's okay to be shy. But you'd be surprised at how good it will feel to talk about your problems and get some relief from them," Valentina said. "I talk to people about their problems and secrets all the time, and they always feel better by the end of the conversation. I might be able to help you with what's going on. Don't you want to feel better?"

The computer geek eyed Valentina and decided that he could trust her. He bit his lip nervously, but then started explaining to her what his issue was. He told her about his lack of confidence with girls and how he wanted to be more comfortable in his personality and body. Valentina listened to him closely and asked good, insightful questions that probed deeper into his secret, inner desire to be more self-assured.

"You want to stand taller in the world. You want to take up more space, and claim the amazing life that you know can be yours. You want a confident life that allows you the power to talk to girls with ease and charm," Valentina said. "Am I right?"

The computer geek nodded with a smile. He was usually very shy talking with any girls, but when he saw the depth of sexuality in her eyes and magnetism, he was literally unleashed by her self-confidence. He stood up straighter and looked her directly in the eyes. He felt like she was bringing up his inner fire from deep inside himself.

"I have always dreamed of being so self-confident and brave that I'm able to speak easily and naturally to any girl I like. I want to be able to express myself and my true feelings to girls. Normally, I feel confused and extremely shy, as I haven't had many successful experiences with females. I'm not even talking about sexually. What I mean is even conversationally, I haven't had much success or luck with females," the computer geek said honestly. "That's why I spend most of my time communicating online. That's how I prefer talking to people. I work online, play games online, and meet friends online. For me, my whole life is online, but I want to find a way to be happy offline. I don't want to be scared and shy anymore. I want to be happy and confident in real life with people face to face."

When he finished his story, he had a red face and could not believe he really told his secret desire to this stranger. Not only was she a complete stranger, but she was a super sexy librarian! The computer geek wanted to leave the library as fast as possible. However, he resisted his urge to flee and waited for Valentina to return with his books. She left with his list of books and soon came back with all he needed to get ready for his exam. She also brought him some motivational books about social communication. Per usual, she wrote a note inside the books with her webcam website, so he could experience her erotic shows and receive healing in that way too. The computer geek took all the books and almost ran out of the library with feelings of shame and embarrassment.

A few minutes later, the director of the library came up to the counter, and again remarked about how easily Valentina pulled out the secret desires from customers. Mr. Morozov reminded her about the sect event tonight and her invitation.

"Tonight is the sect's largest party yet. Every single person who has ever come to the sect will be there. I've been working hard to make it the best party yet," Mr. Morozov said with a grin, as Dark Energy oozed off him. "I have the best drugs and alcohol, so people will be as addicted and intoxicated as possible. Plus, I ordered some new sex toys for people to use. They're going to be so busy trying to drown their sorrows and loneliness in debauchery that I'm going to rob them blind. Tonight's profits will far surpass any money I've made in the past. I can't wait to see the money I make. I want you to come and witness the sect in all its glory tonight. Make sure to wear something sexy. I'll introduce you to everyone as my Goddess who demands to be worshiped and obeyed alongside me. They will grovel at our feet."

Valentina told him that she would join the event, and that she is fine with the sexual dress code. Mr. Morozov was pleased and left to go downstairs to the basement to make sure the event preparations were going smoothly. Valentina was glad to get rid of the director, and she got back to work. She stayed at the library all day and helped a few more visitors with some books. By evening, she left for home so she could put on her sexy, inspiring live webcam show. The sect event wasn't until late, so she had time to perform as usual.

GG Star put on the outfit of a naughty schoolgirl and went on-line where many members and new users were already waiting for her to start. The shy computer geek was also there in the audience. As a computer geek, he was very familiar with working a webcam, and he was accustomed to visiting many erotic websites like this one. He assumed this one would be similar to the other erotic websites he had used in the past, but he was wrong. When the computer geek saw GG Star's show, he was amazed and was almost paralyzed during her magical sexual performance. He was so aroused by GG Star's personality, sexual power, and body. Countless people were enjoying the performance and sent tips. The webcam audience loved GG Star's naughty schoolgirl outfit, as it fulfilled fantasies and dreams from when they were younger.

Somewhere in the middle of the show, GG Star saw the computer geek's username when he tipped her. She thanked him by his username as she looked directly into the camera. He felt like she was looking directly into his eyes and soul. The computer geek invited her into a private chat. GG Star accepted the invitation, and they both disappeared from the public chat. The computer geek was so shy that even typing in the chat was difficult. But GG Star made it easier on him by talking directly to him by voice and eye contact through the camera. She started talking to him and making him feel more comfortable. The computer geek loved the attention he received from GG Star. She asked him questions about himself and wondered more about his life and personality.

Eventually, when GG Star could sense that she should take their conversation to the next level, she asked the computer geek to take off his pants. Because he saw how natural GG Star was and how easy it was to communicate with her, he even turned on his camera and showed himself to her. He took off his pants like she asked. The computer geek started to be braver with conversation, and even asked her to take off her clothes piece by piece. Once she was naked, GG Star played with herself so passionately that her sexual energy hit the guy through the camera and filled him up with sexual self-confidence and satisfaction. Her superpower gave him a sexual charge that satisfied him and gave him contentment.

After her mission with the computer geek was done, GG Star came back into the public chat to say goodbye to her audience members. They sent her a shower of tips for her sexual performance because it gave them satisfaction and emotional healing. GG Star logged out from her website and started getting ready for the sect event. She had an hour to prepare before she needed to leave her apartment. She decided to show up at the event fashionably late because she wanted to strategically wait until all the sect members had arrived, so she could free them all at once. Valentina turned off her computer and got to work.

※

Chapter 19

ENTERING THE LION'S DEN

It was finally time. This was Valentina's most important moment as a superhero yet. If she was successful tonight, she would rescue hundreds of people who were slaves to evil forces and deal a massive blow to Dark Energy and The Great Imbalance. It felt like all her interactions and webcam performances had been practice for this opportunity. With Mother Venus' words of advice and encouragement in the back of her mind, Valentina felt prepared to do what she had to do tonight to save the world.

GG Star put on sexy vintage lingerie, black stockings, red high heels, and a vintage mask over her eyes, so no one at the party would recognize her face. Concealing her superhero identity was of the utmost importance. She also wanted to ensure that Mr. Morozov would not realize who she was. He was an evil and dangerous man, and he would be devastated after the sect was destroyed. GG Star didn't want such a powerful representative of evil and Dark Energy after her. She then covered her half-naked body with a long, light cloak.

Also, to settle her emotional and sexual state, she put a vibrator in her handbag, as there would be a huge number of people at the party and she needed to create a wide zone of her sexually charged energy field. This power should be so huge that it could instantly enter into every person, filling everyone and healing them from the harmful influence of Dark Energy. The sexual energy of GG Star had to be strong enough to give satisfaction and create inner peace and harmony in the hearts and souls of everyone present at the sect. GG Star has never performed a sexy and erotic show in person or in public before, but she reminded herself that she was a magical creation of Gods and the cosmic entities. They gave her a mission to save the world and they equipped her with the superpowers to accomplish her goals. That was why she was sure that she was able to succeed. GG Star looked at herself in the mirror before she left and saw a breathtakingly sexy and powerful woman looking back at her. She was ready.

When GG Star arrived at the library, instead of going in the main entrance like normal, she turned down a side alley to find the secret underground entrance to the sect. There was a bouncer at the door, who let her through. Inside the door, she walked down a set of dark stairs into the basement. Her high heels clicked down the long hallway as she made her way to the final door into the sect. As she approached it, she could hear the loud music blaring. The superhero took a deep breath and quieted her mind, feeling the sexual power and sexual power pulsing inside her. She would soon unleash it in a powerful force, but the time wasn't right.

GG Star entered the sect, and the party was already going strong. Everyone who was invited to come was already there. It was a full house with every single member of the sect. GG Star noticed that everyone followed the elegant dress code and wore a face mask like her. Being anonymous allowed people to go wild and do shameful things they normally wouldn't. Everyone at the party was looking for something. Of course, GG Star knew that this was the wrong place to look for anything, as the director was manipulating them and feeding them harmful substances that faked feelings of happiness and fun.

GG Star made her way to the bar, so she could observe the crowd and everything going on at the party. In different areas of the room, security guards were giving people drugs and alcohol to the point of being inebriated. Some people preferred to mix both alcohol and drugs at the same time for a crazier effect. Everyone at the party, without exception, was doping at their own request. No one forced them. GG Star sensed that these lonely, lost people were so out of touch with their emotions, that they turned to alcohol and drugs to cope and hide from their negative feelings. They did not know how to have fun sober and were afraid of genuine communication with other people, but as soon as they took drugs or drank alcohol, they felt more confident and cheerful. They wanted to communicate and express themselves in public.

On the surface, it seemed like everyone at the sect was happy, but GG Star could see into the hearts and minds of people with her superpowers. The cheerful, fun demeanor was only illusory happiness while the power of doping was at work. People flirted with each other and behaved in a relaxed manner, while they swayed with the power of Dark Energy and their illusions of happiness. They did not realize or did not understand that they themselves exuded a false energy of love and acceptance, which nurtured more and more internal turmoil.

Suddenly, the director of the library appeared on the stage in the center of the hall, and he introduced himself as both the founder and guru of this sect. Mr. Morozov was absolutely sober and looked with satisfaction at his subordinate slaves who brought him a lot of money just to be able to worship him and be part of his sect. He gave an inspiring speech to pump up the Dark Energy in the room.

"Thank you for coming, everyone. It's good to see you all. Some of you join us every night, and some of you haven't been here for a while, but tonight is the party that brings us all together," the director said with a fake sense of hospitality and care. "Here at the sect, we are all one. We're no longer individuals, but part of a whole. We all share the same jolliness in being together, the same wild side when we drink and take drugs, and the same burning in our loins when we let loose and indulge our sexual nature. Now, let's load ourselves up to the maximum tonight with alcohol, drugs, and sex! Do not deny yourself anything tonight. Give in to each and every one of your base desires! Are you with me?"

The crowd cheered with enthusiasm. GG Star could tell everyone felt pressure to appear as if they were enjoying themselves, when in actuality, they were insecure and feeling even more empty inside.

"The sect replaces your family and friends. This is a communal brotherhood and sisterhood where everyone is equal, and I am your leader," Mr. Morozov said. "Tonight I declare a celebration of life! The bar is open for alcohol and drugs, but what's special about tonight is that we're having the biggest swinger party ever! I assure you this path will lead to your emotional recovery and bring you out of the depression in which you live every day. So, grab a stranger and have sex! Enjoy their body and let them enjoy yours. Let the alcohol and drugs flow! Let the sex flow! And of course, let the money flow too!"

The crowd cheered and the director finished his dramatic speech and left the stage. GG Star knew that these lost people would plunge into a pit of despair and rejection of their existence. Artificial happiness had driven people into dependence on Mr. Morozov's sect and everything that happened there. But nonetheless, people listened to his instructions, and as soon as he announced an orgy, everyone began to follow suit. GG Star moved to a very dark corner away from the crowd, and she watched what was going on. She saw how many people were zombified and depressed. They could hardly stand on their feet due to the influence of alcohol and drugs. They did not realize that by their presence in the sect, they followed the rules of the director who acted as a dictator and suppressed their own desires and dreams.

People were so suppressed that they were no longer able to hear the requests and cries of their own souls. They all abandoned their individuality and its manifestation, so they behaved like an unconscious flock of sheep obeying the voice of their leader. The director knew that by, tricking them with the illusion of fraternization in the sect, he would take away their personal identity and turn them into an army of people creating even more Dark Energy. In doing so, he would enrich himself, and all of the people would increasingly become dependent on this imaginary community, promising a false sense of happiness.

GG Star silently watched the actions of the crowd as the concentration of Dark Energy in the hall went off the scale. She sensed that people were unhappy, but they also glad that they would not be alone. They did everything that their leader, Mr. Morozov, ordered. He had called for a drunken orgy and everyone complied. People gradually began to undress, casually touching themselves and their nearest partner. However, they did so without sensuality or any attentiveness to their partner's reactions, especially since all reactions and sensitivity were drowned out by the side effects of the substances. In fact, no one felt pleasure, since everyone was pretending that they liked it. People created a guise of false pleasure and happiness, and even paid for the entire experience. They willingly forked over the money to do so, all for the sake of not thinking or being responsible for their lives. The people at this sect party did not understand that by partaking in this communal orgy, they oppressed themselves and fell deeper into their addiction and depression. This negative decision increased the influence of destructive Dark Energy in themselves and the entire environment.

The DJ changed the music to a more erotic song to announce the beginning of the orgy, and as the music echoed throughout the hall, people congregated into groups and performed sexual acts with themselves and other people. Some people preferred to just watch, but others felt united in the seduction of the group. The people at the sect party touched each other indifferently. They sloppily engaged in sex acts and stumbled around naked. They exchanged negative energy, so they were filled with even more unhappiness. The alcohol and drugs clouded their judgment. Many of the men could not even become aroused due to the amount of alcohol and drugs in their system. It was a pitiful and sad scene altogether. The director watched from the bar with a sick and twisted smile on his face. He knew that the people here at the sect party would wake up the next morning feeling hungover, ashamed, and dirty for all they had done. They would feel even more loneliness and despair, and that hollowness inside their souls would draw them back to the sect the next night, in a never-ending cycle trying to alleviate those feelings. It was a terrible and destructive cycle influenced by Dark Energy.

GG STAR

GG Star decided this was the moment she should use her superpower to stop this toxic process by filling up humans with the healing energy of her sexuality! She emerged from the shadows of the corner. The superhero threw off her cloak and with a confident step, walking towards the stage in the middle of the hall. It was convenient for her to be on an elevated stage in the center of the room, so that her sexual energy charge would hit and have an impact on everyone. GG Star knew what she had to do and she was determined to succeed. Nothing would get in her way.

※

Chapter 20

LIGHT VS. DARK

Her high heels clicked on the stage as she got into position. This was finally her moment to be a beacon of Light Energy and cast out the most concentrated amount of Dark Energy in the city. When GG Star appeared on the stage in the center of the hall, people looked up from their activities. The men and women of the sect paused to see what was happening. They stopped drinking, doing drugs, and engaging in sex, so they could look at the stage. They all wondered who this beautiful woman was in such a sexy lingerie outfit and what she was doing onstage. People in the crowd whispered to each other. Maybe she was a performer that the director hired for the orgy, or maybe she was a sect member who wanted to kick off the party herself. Mr. Morozov was at the bar with his back turned away from the stage. He was greedily counting the money he had made so far that night and had no idea what was happening on stage.

With all eyes on her, GG Star began to seductively move to the music, running a hand over her body and then through her hair. Her dancing awakened her sexual power and joined with her divine superhero essence. She enjoyed herself as she always did when performing. She was confident and powerful in her body, and she exuded the self-assuredness that the lost sect members so desperately wished they had themselves. GG Star's performance was so sincere and natural that everyone around the hall froze and watched her as if under hypnosis! Among the guests in the hall were many library customers who had not yet visited her website, but no one recognized her in the mask, not even the director, who had finally noticed something was happening. He watched from afar, but it was too late for him to stop the performance.

Everyone in the crowd wanted GG Star, and their bodies yearned for hers. They wanted to touch her sexy body and feel the softness of her skin and hair. They wondered what her lips would taste like. However, no one dared approach her because she looked so confident in herself and inaccessible that each of those present did not consider themselves equal to her. GG Star was a goddess to them, who existed in a different, higher realm. She continued her sexual performance, and it became more intense as she felt the erotic music more and more. People could not tear their eyes away from the authentic pleasure on her face, which was so different from the forced and fake pleasure that they had been performing earlier. Her natural, graceful movements showed how extremely in tune she was with herself. This inner harmony and confidence was deeply attractive to everyone who watched. She closed her eyes and seemed to go into a sexual trance. The superhero's strong sexual energy radiated off her like heat.

GG Star finally began to touch herself and soon she achieved a feeling of sexual ecstasy. Just as the erotic music reached its peak, she climaxed at the same time. At the very peak of her pleasure, strong energetic waves emanated out of her from all sides. The waves of sexual energy were very powerful and quickly scattered throughout the hall! These energy waves were filled with an intense sexual charge that penetrated deep inside each guest. Her sexual energy so strongly entered people that even they cried out with pleasure. The entire sect experienced something like a collective orgasm, and their bodies convulsed with pleasure and ecstasy! The orgasm they all felt was so real and genuine, it was miles better than the artificial feeling they had been faking. It was the most powerful amazing feeling they had ever felt, like a burning sun radiated light inside their bodies.

Under GG Star's sexual influence, the effects of alcohol and drugs evaporated from people's bodies and they became sober. The sexual charge overwhelmed the sect members' bodies so deeply that they began to recover from depression and self-doubt. The sexual release flooded them with Light Energy, and it filled the spiritual emptiness in the depths of their souls, healing people from the inside and displacing Dark Energy. In that moment, people found inner peace and harmony. At the same time, they were inspired to live and experience life to the fullest. The people in the audience wanted to create beautiful things. They wanted to travel, come up with a new business, start a new hobby, or ask out the person they crushed on. They were filled with a certain self-confidence that made them want to communicate with others and learn a lot of new things.

Under the influence of GG Star's sexual energy charge, people recovered instantly! It was like the blinders on their eyes were taken away and they could see for the first time. The masks that they hid behind in shame and self-doubt fell off, and they felt comfortable in their true identity. The sect members became whole, and they began to hear the inner voice of their souls. They could hear what she asked them for because her voice was their true desires. People became aware of their heart beating and could distinguish between pain and joy. They could understand what made them happy and what depressed them, and they decided to give up all that brought them down. With the mental and emotional clarity that came from their sexual climax and Light Energy infusion, people suddenly became aware of how damaging the sect was, and they wanted to leave the sect since they did not need it anymore and it did not help them. Everyone wanted to live an inspired life and create beauty and goodness. They were done mindlessly following the director. GG Star had succeeded in breaking the shackles of Dark Energy that the evil library director had enslaved them with! It was a huge victory for Light Energy in the battle to restore The Great Balance in the world.

Mr. Morozov was very angry when he saw how the sect members had been miraculously healed right in front of him. Dark Energy's grip over them disappeared, and they no longer were crippled with self-doubt, loneliness, and depression. They no longer needed to use alcohol, drugs, and cheap sex as a crutch to feel companionship anymore. Members of the sect began leaving the hall in droves once they realized how wrong it was to be there. They put on their clothes, left their drinks and drugs on the table, and made for the exit. Even the bartenders and security guards had inadvertently been healed by GG Star too, and they quit and left their stations.

"Where are you going? Come back!" the director yelled after them. "This is your family, remember? No one outside this hall loves or cares about you and your pathetic life! You may feel better now, but it won't last. You'll come crawling back here like always. Once life deals you a tough hand, you'll crumble and need to drown out your sorrows. The sect will always be here waiting for you."

Mr. Morozov continued pleading with the former sect members not to leave, but he knew it was in vain. He knew they would never come back. Something dramatic had changed inside them, and they had no need for the sect's services anymore. They were happy and free people. He knew that once liberated, a slave does not return to their master. The director slammed his fist down on the bar in anger. He felt a murderous rage and wanted to kill GG Star. She destroyed his business and ruined his evil empire. He suddenly turned toward the stage to find her and exact his revenge, but when he tried searching for her in the hall, she had disappeared.

"Damn!" the director thought to himself. "Who was that cursed woman? She had such power and sexual energy. If only I had seen her true face and that mask hadn't been obscuring it. I didn't recognize her, but something about her felt familiar. I definitely feel like I've met her somewhere before. I remember her energy and personal charm and magnetism."

Moments after GG Star climaxed and sent energy waves throughout the hall that liberated everyone, she quickly slipped out a back door behind the stage. She knew that Mr. Morozov

would be devastated by the loss of his sect business and would want revenge. Before she left though, she glanced back and noticed that for some reason, her superpowers had no effect on the director. She could not understand why, as he was within the zone of her energy waves and she didn't see any protection or barrier that would have blocked her energy. Regardless, GG Star was confident he didn't recognize who she was. Her secret superhero identity was safe.

In the alleyway outside of the library, GG Star put on a large coat that she had hidden earlier. She took off her mask and walked to the street, acting like a normal person out for a late stroll. She smiled to herself. GG Star was very satisfied and happy to help so many people all at once. It was her debut of healing humans personally in public, and she was so proud of herself and her monumental success. She took pride in what she achieved, and most importantly, she learned more about her own sexual power and how to maximize it to its fullest potential. This night, she harnessed and unleashed the biggest amount of sexual energy she ever had before, and she felt enormous satisfaction and euphoria throughout her body, mind, and soul.

Valentina made it home, where her black cat Patrul was waiting for her. She excitedly told Patrul all about her successful infiltration and destruction of the sect, and she thanked him for the special protection hex he put on her before she left. Valentina got in the bed to let her human body rest until morning. As soon as she closed her eyes, she fell into a deep sleep. Once again, she saw Mother Venus in her dreams.

"Congratulations, my child," Mother Venus said to Valentina. "You have made me a proud mother. When all the cosmic entities and I created you, we had faith that you would be a strong warrior for Light Energy. You proved us right tonight. I want to congratulate you on your huge success and the public healing of so many people. Now is not the time to become careless, though. GG Star, you should be very careful as there was one person who was in the sect that was not affected by your superpowers at all."

"You mean the director," Valentina said. "I noticed that he was not healed like all the other people in the hall. I could still sense the Dark Energy swirled inside him and controlling him."

"You're correct. He is still an evil actor and representative of Dark Energy. I'm afraid that because he wasn't affected at all by your blast of Light Energy, which gives us strong evidence that he's not human. No regular human could withstand such a powerful blast of sexual energy and not be healed," Mother Venus said.

"That must be why he always seemed off. His Dark Energy felt different to me, and Patrul noticed it too," Valentina said.

Before Mother Venus left and the dream ended, she reminded Valentina to be careful and stay away from the director. She told Valentina not to worry about her secret identity being compromised because all other people who were healed at the sect party experienced an illusion effect in their brains. This effect made them all believe that their healing occurred in their dreams and not in reality. No one would announce in public about what happened at the sect party or what GG Star had done. Word wouldn't travel in the city, and no one would share information about her with their friends. Her superhero identity was safe.

"That's all, GG Star. Well done and keep fighting," Mother Venus said. "We'll be watching over you."

❋

Chapter 21

AFTERSHOCK

Two months later, Valentina put on a sexy outfit and sat down at her computer. She was going to perform an erotic webcam show for her audience of thousands all over the world. It was a typical night for her, and she looked forward to spreading her healing powers and unlocking the audience's inner harmony through her eroticism and sensuality.

The day after she infiltrated the sect and destroyed the director's evil business, Valentina called into work sick. Mother Venus had warned her to stay away from the director, who was not human. He was some kind of creature who wielded Dark Energy. Mr. Morozov was dangerous, and in order to preserve her secret identity as a superhero, Valentina quit her library job. She didn't think it would be wise to stay employed there with such a powerful evil force because it opened her up to potential danger, and eventually the director would have figured out that she was GG Star. If he did, he would be quick to exact his revenge on her for ruining his sect.

Instead, Valentina continued working on her webcam website, giving people happiness, joy, and a sexual recharge. From her home, she brought them back to life, and people always left the webcam show full of inspiration and motivation. Valentina's superpowers were growing stronger each day, as she saved people from loneliness, unhappiness, sadness, and disappointment. She healed people online during her show, but also during the daytime when she walked around the city. Her sexual superpowers were so strong now that she merely had to smile and make eye contact with a stranger on the street to heal them and rid them of Dark Energy. Valentina overflowed with healing energy, and people were hungry for it and took great pleasure in receiving her healing. Sometimes, she did engage in small talk with people who tried to connect with her, but no more than was necessary for her to spread her Light Energy to them so they felt joy again. In this way, she continued her mission and was ready for any darkness that she came upon in her travels throughout the city.

Sitting in front of her computer, GG Star turned on her webcam and entered the public chat. She told everyone that the show would be starting in a few minutes. She got several messages telling her how excited people were for tonight's performance, but one message caught her eye. There was a private invitation with an offer to join a video chat for double the usual rate and no one else was allowed to join. It was normal to receive private chat requests, but usually they came during her show and not before it started. GG Star accepted the request like she had countless times before. However, the instant she entered the private chat, what she saw stopped her heart in its tracks.

GG Star's computer screen showed the person who had invited her into the private chat. Staring back at her was a slender, middle-aged man who wore a black suit. He was handsome, but his piercing dark eyes were unsettling and revealed evil deep, within him. It was Mr. Morozov!

When he saw GG Star's surprised reaction, he smiled through crooked teeth.

"Hello, GG Star," he said with a snarl, "or should I call you Valentina? That's right, I know who you are and I know it was you who ruined everything for me. You could have joined me and we could have ruled the world in darkness. It's too late for that now. I've been searching for you ever since that night, and I finally found you. There's no stronger motivation than revenge. Watch your back, GG Star, because I'm coming for you, and this time, you won't get out alive."

ABOUT THE AUTHOR

Born in a small town in Siberia in Russia in 1991, Valentina Dzherson learned early in life to overcome any challenges she faced. A determined young woman who knew that she was destined for success, she was accepted into one of Russia's most prestigious faculties for preparing future diplomats, but instead, she decided to study foreign languages. While a student, circumstances intervened and led her to begin a career in adult entertainment. She soon left her native Russia and moved to Hungary where she turned this career choice into her own hugely successful business venture. To the world, she became known as Gina Gerson, one of the most popular and successful adult performers of the twenty-first century.

ABOUT THE ILLUSTRATOR

Rabï Rahmeni, a highly accomplished freelance artist from Tunisia. With an unwavering dedication to his craft, Rabï has carved a niche for himself in the realm of artistic expression, specializing in the intricate art of portraits, character design, and concept art. Proficient in a diverse range of drawing styles, including cartoon, anime, and realistic techniques, Rabï's work exudes a level of professionalism and artistry that captivates viewers.

PRENDE

For these and other great books
visit **HistriaBooks.com**